Half dressed and going for naked...

Starlight Tyler needs to get rid of something inconvenient—like her virginity—pronto. With her mother, a Pinkerton agent, and a wealthy suitor she can't stand on her trail, there's only one solution to stop them in their tracks—Cordero Tate, the love she left behind.

She never expected *his* past to stall her headlong rush into his arms.

Sheriff Cordero Tate is a haunted man on a mission. Come hell or high water, he'll round up every member of the gang responsible for the deaths of his wife and unborn child. He'll make damn sure he never puts his heart on the line again. As in never impregnating another woman. One look at Star, though, and all the old feelings of love and lust come back in a rush. Worse, she's just as determined to lasso him into her web of passion as he is to keep her chaste.

Their exploration of ways around that impasse leads to nights of unbearable sensual pleasure.

Until *her* past catches up with her...

Warning: This story contains several explicit love scenes. If you're offended by such, I suggest you pass on this one.

Other Books by Marie-Nicole Ryan

Hill Country Lawmen Series
(Contemporary Western Romantic Suspense)
Hunted

Loving the Lawman Series
(Historical Western Romance)
Mastering the Marshal, 3
Pleasuring the Pinkerton, 3
Seducing the Sheriff, 1

Music City Heat Series
(Romantic Suspense)
Because of You, 2
Love Me if You Can, 1
Beginnings, Short Story Prequel

David and Miranda French Stories
One Too Many (Mystery/Suspense)
Love on the Run (Romantic Suspense)

FBI Guys
(Romantic Suspense)
Broken Promises, 2
Holding Her Own, 1

Stand Alone Romantic Suspense
Too Good to be True
The Man for the Job
See You in My Dreams

Holiday Themed Short Stories
Valentine's Gift, 3
Pillow Talk, 2
Mistletoe and Mario, 1

SEDUCING THE SHERIFF

Loving the Lawman 1
Erotic Historical Western Novel
By

Marie-Nicole Ryan

RYANDALE PUBLISHING

Copyright

Copyright © 2009 by Mary Varble
Edited by Linda Ingmanson
Cover by Mary Varble

1st Print edition, Ryandale Publishing, 2017
2nd Print edition, Ryandale Publishing, 2019
All Rights Reserved, Ryandale Publishing.
ISBN-

Library of Congress Registration Number: TX 7-386-149

Dedication

To my editor, Linda Ingmanson, who is simply the best.

To all those movie cowboys of the Old West. You kept me entertained for so many weekends.

And to Jody Wallace for all her on-target pre-submission suggestions.

Chapter One

In the far distance of the Texas hill country, Star made out the silhouette of a lone rider headed for the Tyler spread. He sat tall in the saddle and rode like his mama had birthed him there. Even the distance and the yellow dust swirling among the cedar and scrub oak couldn't hide the wide set of his shoulders.

Wide shoulders or not, she was alone on the ranch. Every single ranch hand had left two days ago on the cattle drive to the nearest railhead at Abilene, including her ornery drunk of a father who managed to leave off his drinking long enough to head it up.

She ran inside to the gun rack and grabbed the twelve-gauge shotgun her pa always kept there for shooting rattlers and other varmints.

Maybe it was time for a little target practice.

Varmints—yeah, she knew all about 'em, especially the ones with two legs. Only the ones in Boston wore better clothes, and some of them even spoke politely, but varmints they were, through and through.

She broke down the shotgun and popped in two shells then jammed two more into her pants pocket. She closed the weapon and hoped she hadn't forgotten how to hit where she was aiming.

She eased out the front door and waited in the shadows of the porch before slipping behind an ancient lone cedar. Its trunk was just the right size to conceal her body and the shotg op at the gate. Damned if she wasn't going to melt if he didn't hurry up and state his business.

"Whoa." Sheriff Cordero Tate reined in his horse and stopped at the front gate of the Tyler spread. He pulled off his hat and wiped his brow with his forearm. The dang Texas sun was high at midday and beat down on his head like a sonofabitch. Maybe he was just pissed off because a low-down, bank-robbing skunk, Tom Tyler, had gotten away again. While he didn't expect to run across him at his pa's ranch, it wouldn't hurt to have a look-see.

"Buck Tyler!" Cord called the warning, "Sheriff Tate here!" Caution and common sense went a long way when dealing with Buck Tyler. The man was as ornery as a sidewinder with a headache on his good days. And on a bad one, he was as likely to shoot first and damn the questions. Old Buck was a law unto himself. No wonder his son took up bank robbing.

The sound of a readied shotgun ratcheted though the still, dry air. "Hold it right there. What d'you want?" A woman's voice, throaty and tight with tension.

A woman? Cord twisted around in the saddle, searching for her location. Found her right enough. She peeked from behind the only tree in ten miles and had a shotgun aimed at his head. A frown drew her dark red brows together, but the rest of her was a damn pleasing sight.

Star. Come home at last.

And what the hell was she wearing? Was she supposed to be a woman or one of her pa's cowhands? Blue denim breeches showed the slim curves of her hips, and a plaid shirt didn't begin to hide the swell of her full tits. His cock hardened at the thought of what it'd be like finally to crawl between those long legs and bed her proper. Lord, the nights he'd turned and tossed dreaming about that very thing. He shook his head and pushed the thoughts away. Crawling in bed with the bank robber's little sis was a guaranteed invite for a bullet in the back of the head.

"Well, well. If it isn't little Starlight Tyler. Been a while. Didn't know you'd come home from

Boston. Home to stay, are you?"

"Well, I have, and I am." Her tone was dry as sage brush, un.

Come on. Let me get a look at you.

Perspiration gathered in sticky dampness between her breasts while she waited. Cowboy didn't seem to be in any great hurry. She wiped the sweat from her brow and watched him work his way down the hill and st

each word clipped with a hint of the Northeast.

"Appears to me you've grown up some." He grinned then started to swing his leg over the saddle.

The twelve-gauge didn't waver. "I said hold it." There was an underlying rasp of steel in her tone.

"You don't have any business here."

He stopped and reseated himself. "I'm mighty thirsty, Star. Man can stop for a drink of water, can't he? Where's your pa? I've a mind to talk to him about Tom."

"Pa's not here. Gone to Abilene with the rest of the hands. Haven't seen Tom since I came home."

Her grip on the gun was rock steady. Buck Tyler's son might be a bank robber, but his daughter wasn't. Of the many memories he had of her, it was her redheaded temper that first came to mind. Easy to see she hadn't changed all that much. Might as well test how far she was willing to go. "I'm pretty parched. I need that drink." He stood in the stirrups, swung his leg over the back of the horse and dismounted.

She gave a curt nod toward his horse. "You've a canteen..." Then her expression softened. Her stance relaxed. She set down the twelve-gauge and let it rest against her thigh. Leaning her back against the tree, she crossed her arms over her breasts. "Sheriff Tate? Since when?" Her tone teased as finally she gave him that old familiar smile. "Town must be pretty desperate. When did they start letting young 'uns take on such responsibility. Are you even shaving yet?"

He rubbed his whiskered chin and grinned. "Twenty-five's not that young. Besides, no one else wanted the job. You'd know if you hadn't run off to Boston to live with your ma." He raked his gaze up and down her slim body. "Can't see they citified you much at all."

"Spent four years there. Didn't take to citifying." She gazed off into the distance. "These hills and this valley, not to mention the blazing hot sun, get into your blood. The cities back East are—" She broke off and shivered. "Winters are cold. The chill, it seeps into your bones and kills your spirit. Not to mention, how unfriendly and snooty some of the folks are."

"Lot's happened since you left," he said, not quite knowing how to broach the subject. Marriage, wife and a little baby girl...all dead two years. Yeah, a lot had happened.

"Let's see. My pa's a worse drunk than he was before I left. My brother's a bank robber, and there's no one to run this spread but the foreman and me. And I aim to do it." She nodded sharply. "Say, I thought you were thirsty. Come on. Fill your canteen at the well. Still has the best water in fifty square miles. Might as well give your horse a rest, too. Looks like he's been ridden hard."

"I'll say. Been on Tom's trail nigh onto a week." Reins in hand, Cord led his horse to the trough then followed Star to the well.

Star's hands shook, but she kept them in front of her so Cord couldn't tell how much seeing him after four long—damn long—years affected her. He was a man grown all right, in every sense of the word. Four years older than she, he was a good head taller. His craggy face was darkened by the sun, but the warmth of his dark eyes hadn't changed since the time he teased her at the age of six and dropped a mess of earthworms in her lap in the town's one-room schoolhouse. And sadly enough at one time, he and her half-brother had been the best of friends.

Now they were on the opposite sides of the law.

More important, this Cord Tate with his double six-shooters was nothing like the lecherous lawyer with sweaty hands and unyielding mouth her mother tried to marry her off to back East. Her mama's re-entry into polite society and Star was the price. It'd taken Mama four years to find a man with the right setup—respectability, money, social position—who was willing to take an old maid daughter off her hands.

No indeed.

An unfamiliar stirring of emotions hit her from the moment Cord identified himself. While she might've had a schoolgirl's crush before her mother dragged her along to Boston, what she felt now didn't feel very girlish. Her feminine core clenched at the sight of his long legs and muscular thighs while he cared for his horse before filling his canteen. A man who took good care of his horse would treat his woman with respect, too. But was it respect she wanted?

Never mind what she wanted. She needed a husband and needed one fast before they dispatched someone else to bring her back.

And Cordero Tate fit the bill on both accounts.

"I'm glad you came home. Never dreamed you would." His tone was deep and soft. The richness of it resonated deep within her, turning her into a warm pool of...need? Was there even a word that described how she felt at seeing him again? More than anything she wanted to surrender to impulse and throw her arms around his neck.

Anything to erase her lingering revulsion of Teddy Darwin. She shook her head in an attempt to erase the memories. But none of that emotional stuff mattered. What mattered was keeping to her plan of seducing and marrying Cord as soon as possible. She'd only been home three days. His showing up uninvited and unexpected was an omen.

Every minute counted.

She fluttered her lashes. "My mother—"

"How come she let you come back? I would've thought with her family's connections, she'd marry you off to some rich fellow."

"She tried." She averted her gaze, remembering how the oh-so-upright Theodore Darwin's clammy hands felt on her thighs when he tried to force them into her underwear. She shivered again. Barely an hour after her mother informed her she was engaged to the middle-aged lawyer, he'd tried to force himself on her. Randy old goat—had to be forty if he was a day. Still, she bet it'd be the last time he tried to force a woman without her say-so.

Tears sprang to her eyes as she met his gaze. "I ran away." Twice. "And I'm not going back. You can't make me."

His dark gaze softened. "Darlin', nobody's gonna make

you go back there. Least of all, me. You're home now."

If only it were that easy.

His strong arms surrounded her. She gave in to his warmth and relaxed in his embrace. Her entire body twitched, and all she cared about was the sandpapery touch of his warm, callused hands caressing her.

Quite a contrast to the way old Teddy made her feel. By damn, she'd never let another man make her feel like a cheap whore again.

Cord was her answer. Better than she could've ever hoped. And why shouldn't he marry her? They were in love before she left. Nothing had changed. She could see heat in his gaze. And she'd make him a good wife.

She gazed into his warm brown eyes. "I'm yours, Cord. Why do you think I came back? We were always meant for each other. Make me your woman."

He dropped his hands and stepped back. His eyes widened, and shock scrawled in uneasy lines across his handsome face. He ran his fingers through his hair, blue-black as a crow's wing, a gift from his Mexican mother.

"God-amighty, woman. Have you no shame? Is this how decent women in the city talk?"

The heat of embarrassment flushed her entire body and flooded her cheeks until they were so hot they must've been fiery red. What was it her mama said? Desperate times called for desperate measures.

She stiffened, scowled and dared him to interrupt. "Seems like making me your woman was exactly what you had in mind the night before my mama jerked me onto that eastbound train. Guess you've changed your mind." She whirled and ran for the house.

"Hold on!"

She reached the door first, but he clapped a hand on her shoulder and whipped her around to face him.

"Lot of water under that bridge. You got no idea."

Tears threatening to spill down her cheeks, she glared at him. A burst of fury and a mixture of fear drew her innards into knots. Her heart thundered loud as cattle stampeding headlong toward a sheer cliff.

"No idea? You're the one with no idea. You could've claimed me then. Stopped Mama from taking me away. If you'd just stepped up and said the word, I could've been yours these last four years."

"What and let you pass up the wonderful life you were supposed to have back East? Your ma said—"

"What'd she say?" Star clenched her fists, but at the same time a curl of hope flickered in her belly. "Did she actually stop you...?"

"Yeah, she did. Said I was selfish to keep you here in this backwater. Said I didn't really love you 'cause I was too young and stupid to know the difference between a lady and the half-Mex son of a rancher."

"My mama?" Star straightened her spine and hissed, "In spite of her family connections, we were treated like poor relations. So she tried to barter me off to the highest bidder like a prize heifer. It was her big plan to regain entrance into polite society. I was supposed to marry this despicable man...a lawyer...and he was *old.*" In spite of her best efforts to remain in control, the last came out as a wail.

She rested her head on his chest and sniffed. Against her ear, his heart pounded almost as loud as hers. "I didn't know she talked to you. All I did know was that you didn't so much as come to the train station to say good-bye." She paused and gazed into his eyes. "I cried all the way to North Carolina until she threatened to slap me silly if I didn't stop."

Gently Cord nudged up her chin until her gaze met his. "Darlin', I didn't think I deserved someone as sweet as you." He dipped his head and kissed her full on the lips. His mouth was warm and tender, nothing like the lawyer's. Cord's every touch felt so right. Her body grew heavy with desire. Her knees weakened until she thought she might faint. His tongue swept inside her mouth, and his hands splayed down her back until he cupped her bottom and pulled her close to his hard cock.

Her body grew rigid. She tried to pull away. So, he wanted her, too. But she needed more than a quick roll in the hay...although turning down his overtures didn't have a lot of appeal at the moment. After all, she'd come home to trap him into marriage. It was the only way to keep her mother and old Teddy Darwin at bay.

If she were safely married, this time whoever Darwin sent after her would have no choice but to return to Boston empty-handed.

"So...you want to be my woman?" His tone was raspy and breathless, his breath hot on her neck. "I can't marry you."

"You can't? But you have to. I-I need more." What the Hades was the matter with him? What had she done wrong? Dammit. His hard member was pressing into her belly. She hadn't done anything wrong...yet.

He scowled down at her and adjusted his crotch. "You need more than this, darlin'?"

She scowled up at him. "Yes, dang it. I'm talking something more serious than the size of your...your Johnson."

His darker-than-night eyes glazed over. "Serious? You mean ...marriage?"

"Of course, what else did you think I meant?"

He straightened then stepped back. He shook his head as he held up his hands between them.

"Marriage ain't for me. Not again." He turned and

headed down the steps.

"Again?" Disbelief shoved its ugly face into her heart. She took a deep breath and spit out the

question, "Did you say 'again'?" Dear Heaven, the one time she tentatively broached the subject, her pa had said Cord wasn't married. Why hadn't she stopped to consider he might've married in the four years she'd been gone? Maybe because most Texas men didn't marry 'til later if they married at all. What made him rush down that road?

He whirled to face her, his handsome features hard as stone, his lips a thin, firm line. "Told ya, a lot happened while you were back East. Got married couple years after you left. She died...and our baby with her. Won't take any chances. Not again."

"I'm sorry. I didn't know." But dammit! The past was past. She needed a husband bad and she needed him now. "So, just like that—you're walking away from me. Again?"

He ignored her. She watched him stride to his horse then stop and stare puzzled at his mount. The stallion's cock was hanging low and long. Dang it. Her mare was in season. "You see that you keep him away from my Dolly!"

He turned and glared. The stallion nickered, reared and jerked the reins from Cord's grasp as he tried to mount him. "Shee-it." He stomped the dry Texas dirt then chased after the horse.

Star ran after them. Her mare was in a small corral behind the ranch house, but the fence didn't stop the stallion. With a great bunching of his haunches, he leapt over the fence. The mare nickered and pranced around, lifting her tail. Silly beast didn't know what was about to happen.

She grabbed Cord's sleeve. "Stop him! He's gonna hurt her. She's never..."

"Gotta be a first time sometime...for everyone." He

stopped at the corral fence and shook his head.

His warm gaze drifted up and down her body in as lazy a manner as she'd ever seen then dragged back to watch the horses.

"Ain't no way I'm getting in there and trying to stop anything. She'll be all right. Traveler knows what he's doing."

Dang it. She couldn't keep her eyes off the stallion and his long member. The stallion neighed and scrambled onto her mare's hindquarters. The mare nickered and whinnied with a screech when the stallion entered her and started pumping. Her head whipped from side to side as the stallion kept her in his grasp and hunched over her with mighty thrusts.

Cord chuckled, sidled up behind her and pulled her close to his chest then set his hands at her waist. "I told you he knew what he was doing."

She cocked her head around to face him. "Like his rider—huh?"

His voice was soft and soothing. His breath warm as he exhaled a puff of air on her neck. He ran a thumbnail across her nape, and her knees grew weak, her head arching back against his chest. As much as she wanted to give into the feelings, the questions remained.

She took a deep breath, pulled away from his grasp and spun to face him. "Married? A wife and baby? Lost in childbirth? Must've been awful."

His jaw clenched. "It was. I should've said something sooner. She was shot in a bank robbery, went into labor. They both died. Two years ago, this spring."

"N-not by my brother?" She waited for his answer while her heart pounded as if it would rip clear of her chest. "Please tell me he wasn't the one who killed your wife and baby."

"No, your brother didn't do it himself." The muscles in his face tightened until she thought with one touch he'd fracture and fly into a thousand pieces. "But it was one of his gang. Tommy—he was there, Star, and the lily-livered coward left her lying there, bleeding and dying." He choked out the words then said, "Anyways, just heard talk he was back in the valley. Thought I'd check out your pa's spread before I headed out to his gang's old hideout."

She placed a comforting hand on his shoulder and felt the muscles bunch under her touch. "I'm real sorry, Cord. I had no idea. Honestly, he's not here. I'd tell you if he was."

"Hope you would. But could you really? Turn in a brother to be hanged—don't know if I could in your place."

Hanged? She sucked in a breath and drew back. "But wouldn't he just go to prison?"

"This isn't the namby-pamby East, hon. Out here justice is swift. An eye for an eye."

Could she turn in her brother, actually her half-brother, if it meant his swinging from a tree? "Now that you mention it, I'm not sure I could," she murmured. More likely she'd beg him to leave the country.

Mexico or Canada. Still, the thought of a young woman and her unborn child bleeding to death on the bank's pine floors sent a shiver up her spine.

"You really think you can bring in my brother by yourself?"

He shrugged and slapped the dust from his pants. "Just looking for any sign he's been around. I find something then I'll assemble a posse."

"I don't blame you for being angry and hurt." Truthfully she didn't, but detouring a man from his plans of revenge to thinking about wedding bells instead just made the execution of her plan even more difficult.

Still she had to try. She began tentatively, "I wish I

could've been here for you in your time of loss."

Damnation—she sounded like a simpering fool of a Boston debutante.

"Bad time." He shook his shaggy head. "Don't want to talk about it. Just need to see your brother and his no-good band of killers brought to justice. Owe that to Annie."

"Annie Miller? Is that who you married after I left?"

"Yeah."

"I remember her, the doc's daughter. She was a nice girl, a bit younger than me." Quiet, shy and a little on the plain side. Good grief, how could she think such a thing of a poor woman who'd never done any harm and certainly didn't deserve to die that way...or any other way for that matter.

She reached up and stroked Cord's suntanned cheek. "Careful. Revenge will eat you up from the inside. Is there anything I can do to help?"

He jerked away from her touch. "I'm not a kid with a scraped shin. I'm a lawman and it's my job to bring him in." In spite of his harsh tone, he gently brushed a curl from her forehead. "And your big, green eyes and soft words won't keep me from it."

She blinked. Somehow she had to get his mind to switch gears. "I would never try to keep you from doing your duty to the town, but..."

"But nothing." He shook his head and stomped away to the other side of the corral. He leaned on the corral fence patiently waiting for his stallion to finish his business with the mare.

Once the stallion was approachable, Cord vaulted over the fence, grabbed the bridle, and led the animal around to the front and tied him to the hitching post.

No way was Cord getting away from her. She raced behind him and yanked on his shirt sleeve. "There has to be more to Cordero Tate than the job and seeking revenge.

You need a woman's touch...a woman in your life."

"A woman's touch? That's what you think I need?" His eyes darkened with passion, his voice was more of a growl as he whipped around to face her.

Her touch was exactly what he needed, and she meant to have her way with him.

"You're the one needs a man's touch." He picked her up as easily as if she were a babe in arms and carried her inside the house and set her on her feet.

"My bedroom's upstairs."

"Your bedroom? I'm not taking you to bed. I—"

"I thought—"

"You're not thinking. I could get you with child, and then where would you be?"

Exactly where I want.

She jutted her chin and flipped her hair over her shoulder. "You'd marry me, of course."

"Like hell I will." He shook his head and set his hands on his hips.

Undaunted, she stood on tiptoe, wrapped her arms around his neck and nodded toward the stairs. "First door on the right."

He placed his hands at her waist and walked her backward to the wall and held her there. "I'm not going to make love to you today—or any other." His voice came out raspy and gravelly, full of emotion.

"But you kissed me." She chewed her bottom lip then said, "Your Johnson is—"

He stepped back and held his hands in the air. "For God's sake, stop talking about my prick! No decent woman talks like that."

"But you're still in love with me. I know you are."

"You've been gone a long time, Star."

"I can see it in your eyes." She closed the distance

between them. "You want me. That's all I need."

Besides a husband, that is.

He gave a slow shake of his head. "I don't deny you've troubled my dreams for too many nights. But you need a man who can love you...really love you. Not one like me."

She rubbed her mound against him and whimpered from the burst of heat that shot to her cleft.

He groaned and shoved her against the wall. "You're killing me, woman." His hands shaking, he unbuttoned her shirt and tugged it from her pants. "Beautiful." The word escaped his lips as soft as a sigh.

She arched her back and thrust her breasts closer to his beautiful mouth. His lips went first to her neck. Warm kisses, gentle ones, while he ran his fingers inside the top of the bustier and pulled her breasts free. He laved one nipple until it beaded then turned his attention to the other. Pressing against him, she moaned her pleasure.

He unbuttoned the top button of her pants and slid his hand inside and down there, slipping his fingers up and down her slick wet cleft. She squirmed and arched against the warm touch of his caressing fingers.

"So wet and ready." The words were a rasp of heated breath against her neck as he started massaging her pleasure nub, groaning as he did.

Waves of sensation grew and centered inside her until they exploded in an eddying swirl. Her thighs trembling, she sagged weakly against the wall. "Oh, my stars. Was that supposed to happen?" So this is what being pleasured by a man felt like. What would having his Johnson inside her do?

He stopped and turned his head toward the door. "What—?"

Chapter Two

Then, just barely, Cord heard a sound. Repeated. Knocking snapped him from his brief descent into madness right back to reality. Reluctantly he eased his hand from Stars pants, cocked his head at the door. "Hear that?"

She gazed up at him, her lids drooping with passion. "Hear what?"

He adjusted his prick, willing his urges to subside. "Someone's outside. You expecting company?"

"No." Her eyes widened as what he'd really meant hit her. "Oh, you mean like Tom?"

"Exactly."

"Told you I haven't seen him since I came home. And Pa, he's on the trail drive to Abilene."

"I'll get the door. You—" Barely able to speak, he motioned to her tits. "Do something with those."

"I guess I should. I trust you can hold off the intruder until I pull myself together?" She arched an eyebrow at him and shrugged her freckled ivory shoulders.

A shot of lust kicked his balls. Damn, if his dick got any harder he'd have to take matters in hand. He sure couldn't slide it up her tight little cunny.

No matter how he hankered to do that very thing.

He crossed the main room. Star's quick puffs of breath

told him she was right behind him. Hell, if he couldn't almost feel her breathing down his neck.

"Mr. Tyler, you to home?" The voice was older, definitely not Tom Tyler's.

Cord made out the figure of a man in a derby hat on the other side of the screen door as he moseyed to the door and opened it. "Buck isn't here. What's your business, with him?" God-amighty, of all the folks to catch them in the middle of the day—the Reverend Moore. With a gathering measure of dread, Cord opered the door.

"Well, Sheriff. I see you must've..." The reverend stopped midsentence, his gaze directed over

Cord's shoulder.

He whipped around. Holy hell, the silly woman hadn't buttoned her shirt at all. And her tits were all but popping outta the unmentionable she was barely wearing.

Just like the reverend's eyes were popping outta his head.

Cord blinked and nearly choked on the lump in his throat while the preacher removed his formerly dashing, now somewhat dusty, hat and cleared his throat. "Appears I interrupted something. At least I hope I did. Miss Tyler, I heard you were back and came to invite you to prayer meeting. Not a moment too soon, if I'm to hazard a guess."

"Why thank you so much, Reverend Moore," she said with a wide smile. "Seems like the sheriff thought to welcome me home, too."

What a sassy smart mouth she had. Cord swallowed, his throat dry as the hard-packed yellow dirt outside. How could she stand there half-naked, jawing with the preacher? Shameless hussy.

His shameless hussy.

"Uh, yes..." The reverend sucked his teeth until a little whistle emitted. "Yes, 'twould appear so."

Still smiling, she fastened her denim breeches. "Would you like a nice drink of cold water? You must be mighty thirsty after your long ride out here."

"If it's not too much trouble." The preacher kept sucking his teeth, and Cord felt the sweat slide between his shoulder blades. Lord, how could she carry on like she was acting hostess at a party when dressed in a pair of men's breeches and her tits ready to jump outta her underwear?

He chewed his bottom lip. Even out here in Texas, a woman's reputation could be ruined forever. And make no mistake about it that was exactly what he'd done. He'd ruined her.

"Reckon Miss Star and I are in need of your services, Reverend. I heard she was back, too," he lied, "and we're of a mind to get hitched."

Star pulled on her most innocent expression and smiled. "Get hitched?" she protested, merely for the sake of it. Could things have turned out any better? Some of those beneficent stars she was named for must be aligned just right. "Cord Tate, you ought to ask a woman first before you go and tell the reverend it's a *fait accompli*."

The reverend stopped sucking his teeth and pulled his thin lips into a tight smile. "Well, this certainly shines a different light on things." He reseated his wire-rimmed spectacles higher on his nose. "When would you be desirous for these nuptials to take place?" He dipped his head and eyeballed first Star then Cord. "Sooner, rather than later, would be my guess?"

"Yes, sir." Cord's voice was a croak and sounded dryer than a river bed in a midsummer drought.

The reverend fiddled with his narrow-brimmed hat, turning it in circles through his hands. "Then I'll see you both in church on Sunday morning? Nuptials afterwards?"

"If the Lord's willing and the creek don't rise." All right, she couldn't resist sassing the reverend.

After all, he'd interrupted her education...of a sort. She smiled to hide her insincerity and batted her lashes at her new fiancé. "Guess I'd better fetch that pitcher of water."

Cord cleared his throat, but his gaze cut directly to her chest. "Oh, right." She breezed by the two men, the reverend all smug and righteous as befitted his station. And dear Cord, as uncomfortable as a man in a room full of rattlers. She slipped into the kitchen, her hands trembling as she readjusted her bosoms and buttoned her shirt.

"I'll draw the water," Cord offered from the doorway and headed outside without another word.

Suddenly ashamed to have been caught, and by the reverend at that, she fanned her burning cheeks. Still, it suited her purpose. As much as she'd wanted more from Cord, now she'd have it sooner than she'd ever planned. They'd be man and wife and all his protests about not being a husband to her would vanish like a mirage in the desert.

And added to all the loving ahead, and no small benefit, either, no matter how many men her mother or old Teddy Darwin sent after her, they couldn't touch the sheriff's wife without a whole passel of folks getting up in arms. Her mama and her proposed son-in-law could just go whistle up a rope. Pretending to one and all she was a widow— well, mama could just marry that old goat herself. Probably her intention all along, but once the lawyer laid his leering gaze on Star, he couldn't see her mother as anything other than a deal broker.

Star rummaged through the cupboards with one hand while the other fanned her burning cheeks. Good thing she'd set things to right on coming home, after not finding a clean dish or cup in the whole house. At least now, she could carry Cord and the reverend a drink of water in a clean tin cup each without having to worry about what they'd think of her housewifely skills.

"Here." His tone gruff and purely pissed off, Cord set the water bucket on the scarred pine table.

Her face heated when she met his stony gaze. "Sorry, it happened in such a manner." Even if she wasn't sorry one little bit, she didn't want him thinking she'd trapped him into marriage on purpose, even if she had. He wouldn't be sorry.

She would make him a good wife. She damn well would.

"Couldn't be helped. My own fault I—we— Like I told the reverend, I'll do right by you."

Her temper flared and she spit out the words without thinking. "You don't have to. Nothing really happened."

He backed her against the wall. "What do you mean, nothing happened?" His voice was hoarse and gravelly, and his muscled chest rose and fell rapidly in tune with hers. "I lost my head. Dammit, I was about to lose myself. I had my hands in your bloomers, and I was a heartbeat from slipping my cock in your sweet little pussy. And we got caught. Your reputation is all you have, and I've compromised you. I'll marry you. But understand this, Starlight Tyler, I won't ever be a real husband to you."

She opened her mouth to argue. "But—"

"But nothing. The reverend is waiting for his cool drink of water. Best see he gets it and moves along." His ran his hands through his longish hair, tempting her to do the same. "Hell, now I got to get a shave and a haircut, instead of chasing down your no-account half-brother."

"So sorry to interfere with your plans, Sheriff." She set her hands on her hips and glared up at him. Her heart hammered and her breathing turned ragged. "You *will* be a husband to me. Real or otherwise makes no difference."

"How's that?" His reply came through clenched teeth, the muscle in his jaw visibly jittering.

Oh, yes. He'd be her husband, real and true. See to it, she would. She splayed her hands against his chest then shoved him back just enough to shoulder past him and grab the water bucket. "Like you said, the Reverend's waiting."

Setting the cups on a tray, formerly her mama's biscuit tin, she took the chipped blue enamel dipper and filled the two other cups, one for the reverend and one for Cord. She sure hoped he was set up proper for housekeeping because after four years in Boston she was used to better. Maybe not the finest, but better than battered tin.

In Boston a guest would be offered a cup of tea and tiny sandwiches without the crust. Here in Texas Hill Country, a drink of cool water was the best she could do on short notice.

Ignoring Cord's silence, she pasted a smile on her face and sashayed back to the sitting room where the reverend waited. The good reverend had settled on a rough-hewn chair where his dusty derby rested on bony knees.

"Here you go, Reverend." She handed him the cup then sat on the settee, balancing the biscuit tin-cum-tray on her knees. She shot a quick glance at her brand new, if still reluctant, fiancé. He'd followed her into the sitting room and stood awkwardly, one foot pointed toward the door and one in her direction.

Hm. Undecided whether to stay or go, was he?

If he knew what was good for him...

He took a step toward her—good choice—and swallowed so hard his Adam's apple jumped in his tanned throat. She smiled and handed him his cup. "You must be parched. Why don't you sit a spell and we'll iron out the details for

Sunday."

"Details?" His eyes widened then reason dawned and his face took on a dark tint. Was the shameless and adventurous Cord actually blushing?

"Why, we have to plan the wedding, darlin'."

The preacher cleared his throat. "Well, now, Miss Star, Kenton Valley isn't anything like Boston. I'll make an announcement at the beginning of the service and anyone who desires to attend will stay after the service."

"Works for me." Cord shifted on the settee while one of his knees shook.

Where these two men dimwitted? Set them straight she would. "But what about food? Surely our wedding guests will expect to partake of a slice of wedding cake—doesn't have to be a fancy one. And something to drink? Punch, maybe, or cider? Tea would set a really nice tone for after the ceremony, don't you think?"

The reverend's eyes grew large then he smiled. "Of course, Mrs. Moore brought a fine tea service with her from back East. And her oatmeal cake is admired by one and all in these parts."

"Wonderful," she said. "Simple is always the best way." An oatmeal wedding cake. Heaven forbid anyone served such back East. But she wasn't back East and oatmeal it was.

Reverend Moore stood, emptied his cup and replaced it on the tray. "Thank you for your hospitality. I best head home and let my wife know of the plans. Otherwise she'll have my hide if I wait too long or forget altogether." He gave a self-deprecating chuckle.

Star moved the tray to Cord's knees and rose to escort the reverend to the door. There was much to do...and learn...before Sunday.

Cord shook his head. A woman like Star could be the death of him. No sense of shame. The way she prattled on about wedding guests and cake and punch...

And during all this, all he could think about was her wet pussy and how her scent lingered on his fingers, even now. He stood and carried the tray to the kitchen and set it on the table. He'd have it out with her just as soon as the preacher got on his horse and cleared the property. Yes, he would.

He trudged back into the sitting room and waited in the doorway while she ushered the preacher to his mount and waved him on his way. Like she hadn't been caught with her shirt undone and her tits hanging out.

He closed his eyes. The damp heat of her cunny. Damnation, he could still feel her silken folds as she pressed against him. At the memory, his cock hardened instantly. Adjusting his crotch, he willed his Johnson to wilt. One way or another, she'd be the death of him.

The lady herself returned, elbowing by him.

"Gonna stand there and let the flies in? We've unfinished business." She started to fumble at her shirt as she headed for the stairs.

He planted his feet. "Hell, no! We don't."

She stopped, turned then gave him a lazy smile. "My eyes don't lie. Your Johnson is ready, even if you say you aren't."

Difficult to argue with a sharp-eyed woman. What decent woman looked at a man...down there? Much less commented out loud on the state of his prick?

And he was set to marry her in less than a week? Lord help him, he was in quicksand and sinking fast.

"Nothing that can't wait until we're hitched proper."

She tugged at the top of her lacy undergarment. Her tits

spilled out...white...full...soft tits.

Good Lord! His heart hammered like a miner who'd discovered a bonanza. How would he ever keep from making love to her the way a real husband would? He'd meant it when he'd said the words. But damnation, how would he keep his word with a temptress who was intent on seducing him with every breath she took?

Intent on escape, he looked around for his hat.

"Not so fast." She closed the distance between him and the door, blocking his getaway. "We're officially betrothed. Nothing wrong in sampling the goods...for either of us."

"Ain't fitting."

"Dammit, Cord!" She stamped her foot. "Stop acting like *you're* the virgin."

He took a step backward. The house had a backdoor in the kitchen. "As you should be when you marry."

"Why bother? The reverend doesn't think I am. Let's make it true. If I'm a fallen woman, so be it."

Without warning she grabbed his head and pulled him into a kiss. His blood warmed and his head grew light. Her soft lips parted to his tongue.

Dammit, he lost himself in her heat. His heart pounded like a sonofabitch, so what else could he do but scoop her in his arms and carry her upstairs.

"Good choice," she murmured, her breath a warm whisper against his neck.

Chapter Three

"I knew you'd come to your senses." Star buried her face in Cord's strong shoulder and held on tight while he bounded up the stairs.

At the top of the stairs, he managed to gasp, "Just this one time then we wait 'til we're man and wife."

"Just once? Is once enough?"

"Just once to finish what we started. Has to last 'til Sunday." He set her down on the floor and started undoing the buttons on her men's pants. "So sweet and so pretty. You smell so good, like washing hung out on a sunshiny day."

"Had no idea you were such a poet, Sheriff." He lifted her hair and kissed her neck then left a trail of tiny kisses across her shoulders across her back. She shivered with every touch of his lips against her skin.

"Had no idea you had so many freckles. I aim to kiss every one of 'em."

"Might take all day if you do that. I have another place in mind that wouldn't be offended if you gave it the same regard."

He chuckled. "Just bet you do. But I'm of a mind to take my time." He spun her around to face him. "We'll get there eventually."

Desire mixed with a healthy dose of impatience eddied

through her body in waves. "Never know. We might be interrupted again."

He frowned. "You expecting somebody else?"

She grinned then shook her head. "I guess there's plenty of time if you're not in a rush." His dark eyes glittered with something she'd never seen in the gaze of a man before. It wasn't the sick lust of old Darwin. Nor was it the love of a man for his child.

No, pure and simple it was desire and passion and hopefully more than a bit of love. Emotion surged through her, weakening her knees. What a powerful feeling to realize she could bring so much heat to his gaze.

Never taking his eyes off her, he slowly unlaced her bustier. "You're the most beautiful woman I've ever seen." Once it was unlaced, he removed the bustier. "Women around here don't wear these, unless they're..."

"What? Soiled doves?" Of course he'd know about such things. He was a man. A man whose wife was in the ground these last two years. "Every decent woman back East wears proper undergarments. It's a half-corset. I'm used to 'em. But I hate pantaloons. Knickers fit better under trousers anyway."

"You going to wear those trousers to our wedding?" His mouth curved into a grin as he cradled both breasts in his palms and gently squeezed the tender flesh.

No, she wouldn't wear trousers to the wedding. The very idea. But what would he think if he found out she traveled all the way to Texas disguised as a young man. "They're just more comfortable..." she gasped as he latched onto one nipple and nipped it, "...round the ranch."

He slid the knickers down over her buttocks then gave cupped her naked bottom. "Love your ass. Round and firm—just damn near perfect."

"Just 'damn near'? It's a damn sight better than that.

Careful, I might have to make you pay for that insult." Still, her teasing threat didn't keep her from unbuttoning his shirt and running her hands up and down his flat belly. There wasn't an ounce of fat on the man. Years of riding and working his pa's ranch had seen to that. "I think you ought to get rid of this." She tugged at his heavy gun belt.

Cord straightened, smiled down at her, unbuckled the gun belt and set it on the chest of drawers. He held back a deep sigh. The woman wouldn't be denied. A man made of stone couldn't deny this one.

And only one part of his anatomy could be compared to stone. Before this day was over, he'd have to put it somewhere, but maybe not where she expected.

Still, there was plenty of time before he took his pleasure. Giving her what she wanted was all well and good, but he wouldn't risk her life. Too many good women were buried in the church graveyard. Too many women who died bringing children into the world.

Never. Star was too precious. Couldn't risk losing her again.

Her hands were unbuttoning his trousers and yanking them down to his ankles. He stepped from them and nudged them aside. Her warm, delicate touch, lightly caressing his cock, threatened to make him come.

His breath caught in his throat. "Hold on. Easy. You don't want to do that."

"Why not?"

"Because I'll come and lose interest in finishing what we started."

She cupped her breasts and offered them to him, their small coral nipples tightened into pert nubs. "You'd leave me in the lurch?"

A shudder shook his body. Untutored and still a virgin, yet his Star possessed the instincts of a true wanton. "Never."

Eyes widened and with a seductive smile, she shimmied out of her denim trousers with a wiggle of her hips. "Lesson one?" she asked with a smile that put a dimple in her cheek.

He nodded. "Lesson one. Now, listen to me darlin'. I can't make love to you, not like married folks. But there's other things we can do. Don't want to risk you having a baby."

"What other way is there? I only know one way. And before you think I've done this before, I haven't—b-but I sort of know how it's done."

"Yeah, you saw how it's done out in the corral, but you've got a lot to learn and I'm just the man to teach you." Mouth dry as the desert, he swallowed then collapsed onto the chair at the foot of the bed. He leaned back and groaned. "Darlin', you're killing me. Got me hard as a rock." He reached for her, pulled her down to sit in his lap then slowly loosened the pins from her hair one at a time. She shook her head and let her hair cascade down her back. The silken red mass reached almost to her ass.

"Now what?" Star held her breath while he lifted the hair and kissed the back of her neck, tiny hot kisses that sent threads of sensation pulsing to her nether regions. His breath was warm, and the image of their horses mating in the corral was vivid in her mind's eye. Her core twitched in anticipation. At some point he'd mount her. He'd have to. Her cleft ached with desire to have him fill her. Ride her just like his stallion had ridden her mare.

And just as hard.

He nipped her neck. It was just like the horses. She bent forward, resting her hands on the bed, and wiggled her bottom. Every part of her body was burning hotter than the Texas midday sun. And her nether regions were the hottest of all, not to mention slick and wet.

He backed away from the bed. "What the hell do you think you're doing?"

Shocked by his curt tone, she raised up. "I thought...I mean isn't this how the horses did it?"

A low rumble of laughter broke from his throat.

She let out an annoyed huff. Maybe she was new at this stuff, but she didn't mean to be laughed at.

"What's so damn funny?"

"Didn't your mother tell you anything?"

"Not much. Her goal was marry me off to an old man with hard lips and clammy hands. Said he'd teach me what I needed to know."

"Well, she was right, only I guess it's gonna be me who teaches you."

All right. Just do it. She gazed into his eyes. "That's what I want. I want you."

"Then let me lead, dammit. I know what I'm doing."

She set her hands on her hips and shoved her chin at him. "Yeah, I guess you would. Being an experienced man of the world."

"You talk too much. They teach you to talk smart in Boston?" He pulled her back into his arms. "I like to take things slow and easy. I want you to enjoy this."

Taking great care, he caressed her nipples. Her breasts throbbed; the nipples had tightened into little tingling nubs of need. Next he eased down her knickers until they were at her ankles where she kicked them off.

Reaching for his chest, she found hard muscles lightly covered in dark hair that tapered in a V all the way to his jutting cock. It throbbed and jumped against her belly. Startled, she managed not to show it, and slid her fingers around his length. Smooth like a velvet-covered iron rod.

God. No lie, he was hard as a rock and his Johnson was nearly as big as his stallion's. She whimpered, whether from fear or desire she wasn't sure. But she meant to have it...and him.

He groaned under her touch.

"My God. You're beautiful." He cupped her breasts in each hand and held them while caressing the nipples with his callus-roughened thumbs. Sensations of heat and need shot to her core. Her inner walls clenched. She moaned with the desperation to have him.

He bent his head and sucked one of her nipples, nipping and pulling at it, grazing it lightly with his teeth. Her bones seemed to melt; she sagged against his hard member.

His hands feathered down to her waist and caressed her hips, making her squirm and rub her lady curls against his cock. No man had ever seen her like this, but it was okay because this was Cord and they'd soon be wed. All the time she was in Boston, she never stopped loving him, worrying about him. Her knees began to shake. He tickled her calves and nibbled her knees. He lingered over her legs, caressing them until she thought she'd die from all the heat curling through her.

His slid first one finger then another between her legs, inside her very body, moving them in and out.

Her pussy was slick and wet as she tried to move to his rhythm. More amazing, her entire body burned and tingled as if she were on the brink again. He was going to make her his woman. And he would marry her.

He'd have to.

He licked her belly button and headed down toward her cleft. Her pussy clenched and throbbed with the raging need to have him inside her.

And now. Nothing else could assuage the fire burning and building inside her body.

He picked her up in his arms and carried her to the bed. "Spread your legs. Let me see your sweet little pussy. Let me taste it."

What? Her head popped up from mattress. "Taste it? Are you crazy?"

"Just about. You're driving me that way fast. Now spread your legs."

Smiling she did as he demanded then levered up on her elbows to watch. What was he about to do? He couldn't really be going to taste her, could he?

Well, it seemed he could and would.

Cord knelt on the floor. Gently he parted her silky red curls to find the delicate wet folds and inhaled her tangy musk. Spreading her slender thighs, he buried his face in her pussy. Her female musk was fresh and heady. His cock grew even harder, if possible. He groaned, still unable to believe how responsive she was. He licked all up and down her pussy then buried his tongue inside her, tasting her sweet juices as she squirmed against his face. He thrust his tongue in and out then slithered it up to her pleasure nub, circling it. Sucked that nub and felt it pulse against his tongue. Her thighs trembled and her hips arched to meet him.

She knotted her hands in the sheets and begged him to take her.

He lifted his head long enough to say breathlessly, "No-no. Won't risk it." He dipped his head again and went back to pleasuring her. He lifted her legs over his shoulders and continued licking her clit, while he massaged her breasts and squeezed them gently then tweaked her nipples, teasing them into sharp peaks.

"Come for me, darlin'. Come for me."

Her body afire, Star bucked against his face. Wave after wave of pleasure washed over her until she thought her body would combust. But still he kept lapping her pussy until he took her over the edge. Her sex clenched over and over until tears came to her eyes, and she collapsed weakly against the bed.

"You all right?" he asked softly.

She opened her eyes and gazed into his dark depths. "Was that supposed to happen again?"

"Damn straight it's supposed to happen." His hand eased between her legs, and he slid a finger all the way inside.

Instinctively she squeezed her inner muscles to tighten as his finger moved in and out.

"Easy, baby. There's more."

"More?" she gasped. How could there be more?

"Just getting started."

"Getting started? But you said you wouldn't—you know—put it in."

"You still have a lot to learn."

"Where? 'Fraid my attention was a little lower."

"Don't doubt it a bit." He rose to his feet and set one knee on the side of the bed then slowly lay down beside her. "Maybe I should give you a little break. Too much, too soon can make you awful tender."

She let out a giggle and squirmed, arching her hips, trying to tempt him to do so much more. "I don't want to stop."

He shook his head. "I was afraid of that very thing." He

levered up on his elbow and chuckled. "But Sunday isn't so far away."

"So, I guess I'm still a maid, so to speak?"

"For a fact, you are."

"But I don't want to be." Her voice was thick with emotion. "I want to feel you inside me. I want to feel your Johnson all the way to my soul, and I want to ride you until I come all apart in your arms."

"You've already come in my arms. Coming is coming."

"But I ache down there." She reached down and touched herself. "There must be something...a cure?"

"There is. A real fucking's what you need."

"Yes, that's it." She grinned up at him. Was she really going to say the one word her mama said no lady ever said? Her breath came in short ragged bursts. "I want you to fuck me—like I've never been fucked before."

He reared back against the headboard and laughed. "That wouldn't be hard. Seeing as how you never been fucked, you got nothing for comparison."

She huffed and rolled to face him, worrying her way into the curve of his shoulder. "I cannot believe you're laughing at me in bed. Here I am so hot I'm about to explode like a keg of gunpowder. I'm begging for release and you're laughing."

"Aw, angel, you're a hoot." He nuzzled her hair, her ear lobe, then planted a light kiss on her temple. "You've already had release, as you call it."

"Not enough. And you're changing the damn subject." She elbowed his ribs.

"Oomph!" He pulled away from her, his eyes glittering with passion. "You're a bad girl. You have to pay."

He lifted the hair from her shoulders and nuzzled her neck, sending waves of heat to her sex.

"Darlin', I can't love you that way. Already told you. Not

going to change my mind."

"Dammit. You've done everything there is to do, except that."

"That's all you know. And there you go using curse words. Somehow, I think I'm going to have to paddle your behind after all. Don't you know that girls who misbehave get spanked? And you're a bad girl if I ever saw one." He reached around and gave her buttock a light tap.

Before she could hold it back, a guttural moan escaped her lips. "Tell me why your popping my ass makes my privates throb. Doesn't make a lick of sense."

"'Cause you're a very bad girl. One who could get into all sorts of trouble if you're not careful." He grinned and, without so much as a by-your-leave, pulled her over his lap and started spanking her. Not hard, but not exactly gently either. But her pussy seemed to like it too much, if the throbbing of her walls was an indication.

"Oh—!"

"Told you. Bad girls get spanked. But if she's really, really sorry, this bad girl might get something she really likes."

Her heart racing, she cocked her head around. "Like what?"

"You'll see," he said with a wide grin, "but not today."

"Why not? Surely—"

"Stop." He stood and started redressing.

Dammit. He was supposed to... He couldn't leave now.

"I've stayed here too long as it is." He buckled on his gun belt. "Need to head back to town before my brothers send out a search party."

A sense of loss deep and irrevocable cut into her heart. She reached for his forearm. "Please don't leave me. Surely there's more to lovemaking."

"True, there is." He erupted in a great laugh and slapped

his thigh. "Sometimes I think you're the one who's gonna be teaching me before this is over with." He sat and tugged on his boots and flashed a smile. "We're getting hitched on Sunday. Your daddy would have my hide if he knew what we've been up this day. Wouldn't be a shotgun wedding. No sir, it'd be a shotgun up my ass and the trigger pulled."

She made a face, and frustration sharpened her tongue. "Guess it's a good thing my daddy's on the cattle drive."

"Damn straight."

She bent over and jerked on her knickers then snatched the bustier from the chair and pulled it on, lacing it as best she could. "At least there's no chance of getting with child."

"Nope."

She shrugged and smiled to herself. But if he thought they were gonna be husband and wife and not ever get around to making babies then he had another think coming. She'd be his wife in every way, even if she had to liquor him up. And once he and his big old cock found their way home, he'd never leave her.

And her mama, Teddy Darwin and all the Pinkerton agents in the U.S. of A. could just go piss in the wind.

"Still wish you'd stay."

He stared down at her, his gaze warm and lingering. His muscled chest rose and fell with each breath. "Have to go. I'll try to come back and check on you. Otherwise I'll see you on Sunday."

"No!" She barely managed not to stamp her foot. "That's five days away." She buried her face in his chest and rubbed her pelvis against his cock. Reassuringly it hardened and pressed into her belly. "Now I know what I'm missing, I don't think I can't wait that long."

She glanced up and grinned. Poor fellow. He'd shut his eyes as if that would keep his resolve strong.

"I'll be back this way by Friday at least. I promise." The

last came out with a groan.

"I might just make it until then." She tiptoed and aimed for his mouth. Hit his chin. Then he smiled, inclined his head and slanted his mouth across hers. Kissed her hard. Kissed her soft. Kissed her every way between. Man had the mouth of an angel, or was it a devil? Her knees weakened—damn, they were doing that a lot lately—and she grew as dizzy and faint as if she hadn't eaten for days.

Knowing he would catch her, she sagged in his arms.

He stepped back. "None of your wily tricks, missy. I'm on to you."

"I like you better..." she stiffened her back and set her hands on her hips, "...when you're busy loving me."

"Careful or you won't see me 'til Sunday morning at the church."

"Better see you before then." Her bottom lip stuck out in a pout. "You're leaving me high and dry."

He shook his head and laughed, as if surrendering and admitting her hold on him. "Okay, you little witch. More likely sooner than later."

She gazed up and fluttered her lashes. "Tomorrow night, maybe?"

"Maybe."

"I'm all alone out here." She gave a pretty pout. "Never know what might happen to a woman all alone."

"All right. If I can." He leaned down and kissed her forehead. "Provided there aren't any holdups or shootings in town requiring my attention."

"I'm pretty sure I'll be requiring your attention." She gave an exaggerated pout. "Your *undivided* attention."

"And no doubt you always get just exactly what you want."

"I intend to, starting today." She gave a sharp nod, assured she would definitely wed this man. And he *would* be a husband to her.

In every way.

Cord kissed Star one last time, slow and deep. As much as he hated leaving her for even one night, he had to. Just knowing she was back had set his head in such turmoil, because there were too many things that could go wrong if they were together. He'd lost her once and he couldn't risk losing her again. But he'd stepped forward and told the reverend they were going to marry. And they would.

Having once tasted her, he needed her sweet loving like an opium eater needed his pipe.

Chapter Four

The next morning, Star dressed early and hitched her mare to the buckboard. The countryside passed in a blur. All she could think about was Cord's making love to her over and over.

Before she could play out the memories of each touch and word, she reached the town of Kenton Valley, population three hundred and forty-seven. She stopped in front of the general store, hopped down and tied the horse to the hitching post. Hands on hips she stared up at the fading blue and white sign. The hot Texas sun hadn't done Wheaton's Mercantile any favors since she'd last been in town. In fact the whole town was smaller, duller and dustier than she remembered.

Removing her shopping list from her pocketbook, she gave a sigh. It'd been a long time since she cooked a real meal, never one all by herself. Her uncle in Boston had servants and wouldn't hear of her entering the kitchen like a common servant. Hopefully her cooking skills weren't too rusty. Keeping it simple was the trick. Somehow she'd come up with a decent meal to feed Cord if he came for supper. And something told her he would. And afterwards...

She checked the small timepiece pinned on the bodice of

her shirtwaist. She'd have to hurry if she was going to get back in time.

Unable to resist, she darted a quick look down toward the sheriff's office. No sign of him anywhere. And she'd hoped to catch a glimpse of him. Better he caught one of her. Jog his memory if it needed it.

"Looking for me?" Cord's deep voice came from behind her.

Surprised, she spun around and sputtered, "W-why would I be looking for you?"

He grinned and lifted his broad, broad shoulders in a shrug. "Don't know. Just figured you might."

"You 'figured' I'd have to come to town today? I assure you I'm merely doing my weekly shopping. But if you wanted to drop by around supper time, you might find something good to eat."

"Long as you promise not to poison me." His luscious mouth lifted in a broad smile, setting her heart to beating faster than might be healthy.

"I'll have you know I'm not half bad as a cook." She grinned. He wanted to kiss her. She could see it in his eyes. "Just haven't had a chance or anyone to practice on...lately."

"Now that brings to mind other things than cooking. So I'm coming to supper."

"I thought you might. Hoped you would anyway."

"Hadn't you better get a move on? Reckon I'll be hungry. Real hungry." He let out a chuckle, and his eyes shone as he teased her.

She chewed her bottom lip and felt her neck and cheeks heat up. "Bring your biggest appetite, because I'm starving already." It was all she could do to keep from throwing her arms around his neck and rubbing her body all over him.

"Careful, darlin', we're not alone here. Wouldn't do for

you to take advantage of me right here on Main Street."

"Me? You—" She poked his chest, and he started laughing and shaking his head.

"Gotta head out and meet the stage, and see that brother of yours and his gang don't have any fancy ideas about robbing it." His mouth twitching as he loomed over her, one hand rested above her head on a weathered turned column. "Must say it's a real pleasure seeing you in town."

"Nice seeing you, too, Sheriff." She curtsied briefly as if she were on a Boston street and meeting a proper gentleman. In the distance, she spied two women with their bonneted heads together giggling.

"Don't you pay those old biddies any mind. I'll see you for supper." He swept off his cowboy hat and bowed.

"Stop that. You're making a spectacle of yourself...and me."

"Can't have that now, can we?" He strode away laughing, but the two women stopped their giggling and scurried off in the opposite direction.

Laughing. The man was actually laughing at her. And so were those women.

Opening the door, she swished her skirts and stepped over the store cat, who rolled over on his back, gazed up at her with wide yellow eyes and yawned.

"Same to you, Buster," she said with a grin then crouched down and stroked the soft yellow fur on top of his head. "At least you don't pretend to be anything but a fat cat who lies around all day in the sun. There's a certain man who could take notes if he were smart enough."

"Ahem." Abner Wheaton, the proprietor, stepped around the counter and smiled, showing uneven, rat-like teeth. "Miss Tyler, I heard you were returned safely...from Boston, was it? What can I provide you in way of comestibles today?"

His words were civil enough, but the knowing, almost insolent speculation in his gaze sent a sick shiver through her entire body. She stiffened her back and gave him what she hope was an imperious expression. "Yes, I'm returned home for good." *Not that it's any of your business.* "It's a fairly uncomplicated journey these days—what with the railroad and all."

"I hear there are upcoming nuptials?" He licked his lips in a dainty catlike fashion, the tip of his pink tongue barely visible through his sharp teeth.

Her jaw clenched as she bit back the inclination to tell him to mind his store and not her. "Yes. Although how my impending marriage affects you I can't imagine."

"I—uh, suppose the wedding is..."

Of all the nerve. "This Sunday after services." What had the pastor done? Had he spread more than the news of the marriage?

"Best to take no chances that way." He nodded knowingly, his rat-like teeth biting into his lower lip.

"Pardon?" She kept her tone imperious and crisp. "Now if you have no additional impertinent questions or personal comments, here's my list. Please have them loaded as soon as possible."

Tilting her chin upward a notch, she turned and, taking care not to tread on the cat, marched from the store. Her face still flushed with anger and more embarrassment than she ever thought possible, she bumped elbows with the solidly built woman entering the store.

Oh, no. The preacher's wife. "Pardon me, Mrs. Moore. I didn't see you. Good day."

The woman's eyes widened, her mouth opened and her chin wobbled before she could speak. "M-miss Tyler, I'm must say I'm surprised, nay, shocked to see you out and about."

"I'm sure I don't know what you mean. I'm afraid my father has let the ranch run down terribly in my absence, so I'm here to restock." Surely if she went about her business as if this were any other day, everyone would soon forget about any rumors the good reverend had spread in advance of her wedding.

Normally a good-natured and pleasant woman, Mrs. Moore froze, her expression changed into a frown of outright disapproval. "'Tisn't right. I'll have to have a word or two with your father."

The woman's entire body seemed to shudder as she brushed past Star.

"Afraid you'll have to wait until he returns from the trail drive. Good day." She nodded and tried to swallow, but couldn't. Her mouth was as dry as the fine yellow dust, ever present in the air. So this was what it was like being the object of gossip and knowing glances. Tears stung her eyes. She blinked them back.

Maybe what she needed was a short walk down to the sheriff's office. Without a doubt, she wished a certain lanky lawman had stuck around a little longer. Feeling small and ashamed wasn't a part of her nature, but she'd fallen prey to the storekeeper's prurience and Mrs. Moore's disdain anyway. Would anyone else treat her any better? Who did these people think they were? She was one of them from birth, but in the meantime they'd grown petty and small. Or had they always been this way and she'd been too naïve to notice?

Could she live her life like that—on the outside of everything she loved about Texas? While Kenton Valley was far from high society, she dreaded running a gauntlet every single time she came to town. These were people she'd known all her life. Facing censure with every look, every slight, or every mocking smile wasn't how she wanted to live her life.

Cord had been right all along to tell the reverend they were going to get hitched. He knew these town folk better than she.

Dammit.

By the time Star made the short walk down to the sheriff's office, she'd heard, but ignored, the catcalls of several old farts who had nothing better to do than chew tobacco, spit and take up space in front of the feed store and barber shop.

Finally she reached the office where the man she loved had better be on hand to accept her request to walk her back to the buckboard.

One of his brothers, Nash, looked up when she opened the door and grinned. "He's not here. He and Luis headed out to meet the stage, just in case—"

"I know. I saw him before he left. I was sort of hoping he might still be here." Her bottom lip trembled. She'd run the Main Street gauntlet for nothing. All for nothing. Now she'd have to walk by those old coots again and listen to another round of their lewd comments and gestures.

His brother sprang up from his chair, his long, lanky body movement awkward like those of an unsteady colt. "Have a seat, ma'am. Is there anything I can do? Drink of water, perhaps?"

From catcalls on Main Street to Cord's anxious and over-solicitous brother, now that was quite a contrast. "No, I'll be going." Hesitating, she bit the inside of her lip and fiddled with the beaded fringe on her purse. Should she leave a message? "Tell him...I stopped by. That's all."

"Surely will, Miss Star."

She turned to leave and the memory of those raucous

catcalls stopped her. Turning to Cord's baby brother, she smiled. "Would you mind accompanying me to Miss Nelson's dry goods? I still have to purchase some fabric and some sewing notions...for my dress."

He flashed a wide grin and offered his arm. "Glad to."

"I appreciate it, Nash. I really do."

"Anything for my sister-in-law—almost, that is."

Her face heated a bit, but she managed a grateful smile. "Thank you. Now did you mean I'm almost your sister-in-law or you'll do almost anything for me?"

"You know what I meant." Her almost brother-in-law gave an evil sounding chuckle. "You're playing with words, trying to catch me out."

"Not really. Just teasing. Isn't that what almost sisters-in-law do?"

"You're my first almost—" He broke off and cleared his throat. "No, that's not quite right."

"It's all right. I was sorry to hear about Annie and the baby, but I'm sure she enjoyed being a part of the Tate gang."

The young deputy blushed and pulled at his collar. "She was a sweet gal. Y'know, that was a real bad time for Cord. All of us."

"I'm sure it was." Growing more uncomfortable by the minute, she suggested, "Maybe we should go?"

"Sure." He grabbed his hat from the rack and settled it on his head.

They walked by the catcalling old farts, but Nash's stern expression and his grim salutation,

"Gentlemen," silenced them before they could humiliate her again. When they reached the dry goods store, next door to Wheaton's, he opened the door and ushered her inside. A tiny bell jingled overhead.

She inhaled the unmistakable smell of new fabrics and

linens and let out a sigh of relief.

Nash turned to leave then stopped and grinned. "I'll tell my brother you came by."

"Thank you, Deputy," she said, keeping her tone formal since Miss Selma Nelson, the proprietor, rushed into the store proper from a back room, brushing lint and short remnants of thread from her gray shirtwaist. Her complexion was fair and clear, as were her startling pale gray eyes fringed with long dark lashes. The dressmaker's honey brown hair was drawn back into a tight bun. It appeared as if her tresses wanted to spring free and wave down her back. Why would this slender seamstress hide her greatest glory, thus downplaying her true beauty? Perhaps, she didn't want to outshine her customers.

"My goodness, Miss Tyler." A wide smile spread across her usually stern visage. "It's been such a long time since we've seen you in town."

"Yes, I've been away, but now I'm in need of a dress, something simple yet special. And I'm afraid I'll need it by Sunday."

"Yes, of course. I heard the wonderful news. I'm so happy for you and Sheriff Tate. But surely you brought many fine things from your stay back East?"

"No. I traveled very lightly." Very lightly indeed.

The seamstress walked over a counter and pulled out a bolt of pale green fabric sprigged with tiny yellow flowers. "This would be perfect with your hair and eyes. What do you think? Maybe some nice lace trim, too?"

"It's lovely. What about a dress pattern?"

"Here, let's have a look in the style book and you can tell me which one you favor. Taking into consideration the ceremony is Sunday, we'll need to keep it simple. I don't suppose you have a dress form?"

Star shook her head. "No, but I can help with the sewing

if you can do the sleeves—I'm no good at setting-in sleeves. In fact, why don't you ride back to the ranch with me, and we can start work on it together? I have the buckboard here. We could load your dress form in the back of the wagon with my provisions and..." She paused. "Wait. How will I get you back? I have to cook supper tonight for company." Now that sounded like she was trying to give the seamstress the bum's rush. "You must stay for dinner."

"Oh, no, dear. I couldn't intrude. I have my own conveyance—a smart little buggy all the way from—uh, St. Louis. I inherited it from my uncle—he was a doctor—when he passed away last summer."

"You're still welcome to stay for dinner. It'll just be my intended and me."

Miss Nelson laughed. "Now I absolutely know I won't intrude on your privacy. Tell me, has your father been apprised of your plans to marry?"

Star's cheeks started heating. "He's away on a trail drive, but I expect him home any day now. I suppose you think me brazen to be all alone with my fiancé."

The seamstress shook her head. "In my position I learned a long time ago not to judge people. I've kept a lot of secrets in my time and hidden a lot of bulging waistlines with my clever sewing." She stopped and chuckled. "If you only knew—but that's not important. A woman has hard enough time in this man's world without other women giving her a hard time."

"I wish more folks felt that way." She glanced around the small store. "Won't I be taking you away from your business?"

"So what? It's my shop, and if I want to close it long enough to visit a friend and help her get her wedding dress ready, I will. I answer to no one but myself and my customers. And right now you're my customer."

"I sort of like the sound of that—answering to no one."

"Not having second thoughts about marrying our fine sheriff, are you?"

"No," Star giggled, "but I still like the sound of it just the same." No way would she ever regret being in Cord's arms every night for the rest of her life.

"All right then." The seamstress rubbed her hands together. "I'll this fabric cut off the bolt, and while I'm doing that, you pick out the thread and lace and anything else that suits your fancy."

She nodded and wandered over to the lace counter. "White or ecru? Which do you think best?"

"Keep looking. There's some pale green French lace I've been wanting to use for such a long time and just never had the right dress or person for it."

"This one?" Star held up a card of pale green.

The seamstress nodded. "Yes, that one."

Holding back a smile, Star shivered. Was she really going to marry Cord in only four more days? She'd be safe forever. Sunday couldn't come fast enough.

After they stowed the dress form in the back of the wagon with the rest of the provisions, Star waited until Miss Nelson brought her buggy around. A smart, black buggy it was, too. "Ready?"

"Sure enough." The seamstress flicked the reins and took off in the direction of the ranch.

Star wheeled her mare and buckboard around, and headed after the black buggy. At least there was one person of the female persuasion who didn't judge her. Of course, Cord's brother had proven himself a perfect gentleman, too. What would it be like to be surrounded by caring and loving men like Cord and his two brothers? As far as she could tell, all three of the Tate boys were fine men, good and true.

Not a bank robber or a drunkard in the entire lot.

Chapter Five

Star wiped her hands on her apron and experienced a great feeling of satisfaction. The chicken was cut up, dredged in flour and already sizzling in the iron skillet. Thank God, Miss Selma Nelson had come and helped her with the wedding dress. Poor woman had no inkling she'd have to wring a chicken's neck because Star was too squeamish to do it. Plucking and cutting it up were bad enough. Honestly, there were a couple things about Boston she missed: a cook, for one.

Snapped green beans, cooked with bacon, had simmered all afternoon. There were biscuits browning in the oven, having taken the place of a homemade apple pie, and for the moment, potatoes boiled briskly on the cook stove. Miss Nelson had left not ten minutes earlier after declining Star's second invitation to stay for supper. "No fifth wheel on the wagon for me," the good woman said and took off in her smart, little buggy.

Bless her heart.

Considering none of her fine supper, not counting the chicken, was produced by the ranch, she'd done the best she could. No one had taken care of the vegetable garden or done a lick of canning while she was back East. Everything on the table came from the general store. Next year she'd get an early start and clear the garden for planting and see the ranch hands had something to eat besides beans. Honestly, men were useless without a woman around to make a home.

No, wait. She'd be living with Cord next year. Or would she?

She wiped her floury hands on her apron then checked her timepiece. Getting close to five. Just enough time to make the milk gravy before Cord arrived, ready for his supper.

What would it be like, cooking dinner for Cord every night and making slow, sweet love afterwards? She shut her eyes for a second, remembering his caresses and her responses. The man could certainly make a woman feel like she was drowning and desperate need of coming up for air whenever he merely looked at her. But his touch... "Ah..."

"What's wrong, darlin'? You remembering how it was with us?"

Her lids popped open. Cord, in all his male glory, was standing in the doorway. His hair was slicked back, and he was wearing what had to be his Sunday-go-to-meeting suit. One of his hands was suspiciously hidden behind his back.

"I wish you wouldn't sneak up on me all the time. It's very unnerving."

"I brought you something." From behind his back, he produced a small bouquet of wildflowers and purple sage. "A small gift for my hostess. Isn't that how they do it in Boston?"

"Yes. Yes, it is." Good Lord, was there anything resembling a vase on the entire ranch? She reached for the flowers, still not sure what she'd do with them.

"No, you don't." He snatched them back and with his free hand pulled her close.

Her heart pounded, sending the warmth of a flush up her neck and to her cheeks. A very different kind of heat curled its way to her lower belly. "Better watch those hands of yours. I'll have you know this is my first real home-cooked meal since coming home. That's not including the pot of beans and stew I've managed to burn the other night." She wrung her hands and reached again for the flowers.

Damn the man. He had her insides quivering and her knees knocking.

She glanced down at her blue-bell flowered cotton shirtwaist. Good thing she'd worn a dress instead of the usual denim trousers. At least her knocking knees were hidden from his too observant gaze.

He pulled back and gazed at her quizzically. "Nervous? Cause you're talking faster than I can take it all in."

"Nervous? Not at all. But you should know my cooking's on this side of rusty."

"Smells mighty good to me." He craned his neck to see what was on the stove. "O'course appearances could be deceiving. You're not going to poison me, are you?"

"Lord, I hope not." Again she reached for the bouquet.

"Nope." He held the wildflowers high over her head and waggled them back and forth.

"Blast you, Cordero Tate. Give me the damn flowers so I can put 'em in water before they wilt."

"Maybe they're for your father." He leaned against the door jamb, a lazy grin spreading across his rugged face.

She set her hands on her hips and reined in the very strong urge to smack him. "You said they were a *hostess* gift, and besides, he's not here."

He squinted and shrugged his broad shoulders. "I did say that. Didn't I?"

"You're worse than a child playing games."

"This game's a lot safer. If your pa was to come home and catch us playing any other kind of games, you might end up a widow woman before you're a bride."

His tone was hushed but left Star with no doubts about what kind of "other games" he had in mind, especially since they were the same ones she had. "He's still not back from the cattle drive, and I didn't make enough for him anyway." She shrugged then gave a hop, snatched the bouquet and ran to the sink with it. "I have to put these in something. It's not like Pa bothered to keep house while I was gone."

"Maybe his heart was broke, like mine."

He'd come up behind her. Her hands started trembling, but she turned to face him. "Like yours?"

"Yes, when you left. Now I know you didn't have a choice."

"I'm back now." Not wanting him to read her thoughts— something he seemed to do at will—she, averted her gaze, hunkered down and searched under the counter for a vase or pitcher.

"Yes, you are. And I surely am glad. I missed you. Why do you think I—?" He broke off, shaking his head.

"What?"

"Never mind. What time's supper going to be ready, woman? Don't you know a hungry man when you see one?"

There it was. She pulled a pitcher from the lower shelf. "This'll do for the flowers." She straightened to find him almost on her heels. Elbowing him out of the way, she said, "A little crowded in here, don't you think?"

"I can take a hint. Now that you have my flowers, you think you can just shove me out of your way."

He took the pitcher from her. "How about I draw some water?"

Speechless, she nodded. Damnation. Never in her life had she ever wanted a man like she wanted this particular aggravating one. Wanted him in every way a woman could want and need a man.

He set the pitcher aside on pine counter. "Maybe those flowers will last a few more minutes." He slanted his mouth over hers and kissed her hard. His tongue swept inside and plundered. All her bones turned to overcooked mush. Her arms went around his neck and he caught her as she sagged into his arms.

"I've missed your arms and your mouth and—"

"—and? What else have you missed, darlin'?"

"All the wonderful things you do to me, and I just wonder when you're going to teach me some way to pleasure you?"

"Plenty of time for that, gal." His stomach growled and she was close enough to feel it.

"You are hungry, aren't you?"

"Afraid I am. And one thing my mama taught me was to eat food when it was hot and to clean my plate."

"Then I best hurry and fill your plate because there's more to tonight than eating supper."

He chuckled and pulled her to him for a quick kiss then swatted her behind. "Get busy, woman."

Smiling, she quickly filled two tin plates with helpings of food. No fine china or serving pieces, but more than likely her guest didn't care. Surveying her handiwork, she gave a sigh of relief. At least the food looked and smelled delicious.

And she hadn't burned a single thing.

"Supper's on the table. Tuck in." Her mother would be horrified at her manners. Yes, she could sell her daughter to the highest bidder, but then her mama's manners were always above reproach. Of course when it came to literally selling her daughter to an old creep like Teddy Darwin, that was another matter entirely.

Cord pushed back from the table. "Mighty fine supper,

ma'am. Can't say I've had better in quite a while. He rose and scooted his chair under the table then grinned at Star. "Want some help with those dishes?"

Her eyes widened as if his suggestion surprised her. "Sure you won't mind a little woman's work?"

"Sooner you get done, the sooner we can talk and the sooner we can..."

"You're so right, Sheriff. I cannot help but agree."

"'Bout damn time you agreed with something I said."

Together they made quick work of the cleanup. She washed. He dried then folded the dishtowel and laid it on the counter. "Come on. You've put me off long enough." He took her by the hand and led her into the sitting room, his heart pounding loud enough to be heard in the next county. Was he really about to do the one thing he swore he'd never do again: get hitched? But he had to and not just because of what folks would think. His brother had told him about having to escort Star in order to protect her from the old drunks who congregated along the street.

Dammit. He loved the woman. She'd bewitched him when he was a seventeen-year-old kid. And now, all these years later he was under her spell more than ever. Living without her wasn't an option.

She walked over to a kerosene lamp and lit the wick then adjusted the flame. While he watched, she sashayed to the settee and sat then proceeded to arrange her skirt carefully over her knees. Looking up at him expectantly, she smiled, somewhat ironically, one eyebrow arched.

He sat beside her—more like he perched. Should he kneel first? Aw, hell. Proposing never got any easier, no matter how many times a man did it. He swallowed the big old lump trying to form in his throat.

"Now what on earth do we have to talk about? I'd much rather just go upstairs." She fluttered her lashes, thick, dark copper-colored fans.

"Will you just shut the fuck up!" He scraped his hand back through his hair.

Star's lashes stopped their incessant fluttering and widened, revealing her green gaze was filled with confusion and more than a little anger. "You will not ever speak to me like that again or I'll shoot you myself."

She popped off the settee, ready to run, but he grabbed her wrist. "Please don't go. I'm sorry. You've got me in such a state I don't know what I'm saying half the time."

She paused. "Is that so?"

Damn, the woman's tone was cool enough to freeze a man's *cojones*. "Sit down and just listen to me."

"Then stop ordering me around like I'm one of your prisoners."

"If only..." he muttered quietly then added quickly, "...I didn't mean that. Please, will you just sit down and let me say my piece?"

She looked down her perfect freckled nose and let out a sigh. "I suppose, since you rephrased that arrogant demand to a polite request." She sat and folded her hands in her lap.

He stood then went down on one knee, something he didn't even do for his first proposal. "Starlight Tyler, will you do me the honor of becoming my wife?"

She turned her gaze toward the beamed ceiling, first in one direction and then another then finally back to him. "Is that it?"

"Is what it?"

"That's all you have to say, just a bald proposal? No 'I love you more than life itself' or whatever it is that a man should say to the woman he expects to spend the rest of her life tied to his side?"

"'Tied to my side'? Is that how you see being married to me?"

"Maybe I'm too romantic, but I don't want you to ask me out of fear of my pa or because you think it's the right thing to do."

"Dammit, woman. I love you like I've never loved any woman in my whole life."

Chapter Six

"That's better. Go on." Rather than gaze into his eyes, Star perused her folded hands. At least they weren't visibly trembling, even if on the inside she was shaking like a leaf in a windstorm. She had no intention of refusing his proposal, especially not after the way she'd been treated in town that morning. Still she needed to hear him say the words. Likely it would be the last time Cord ever called his romantic side to the fore.

"But you're the most aggravating female I've ever come across."

Aggravating? Well, so was he. "Fond of taking one step forward and two back are you, Sheriff?"

"I've kissed your sweet lips. I've seen every inch of your body and licked the juices from your sweet pussy. You're a hell of a woman, and I don't know if I can handle you, but I'm willing to give it a hell of a try, 'cause I can't imagine spending the rest of my life without you at my side. Not tied, but there with me because we belong together. Dammit, woman, I stood up and saved your reputation when the reverend caught us. I love you. What more do you want? My blood?"

Star slipped from the settee to her knees. Face-to-face, she gazed into his warm brown eyes. In the dimly lit room his love shone in his dark gaze. She licked her lips before she spoke. "Normally your heart would be sufficient, not that your blood would hurt this tattered old rug." She glanced down at the rag rug pieced over a generation ago. "But I must have your promise that you'll be a true husband to me in every way."

His jaw clenched. He averted his gaze from hers.

She reached for his chin and forced him to look at her. "Don't turn away from me. Cord, I want to bear your children. Tall, strong sons to carry on when we're too old. And beautiful daughters who'll find their own true loves. Otherwise..."

She held her breath. Did he love her enough to accept her conditions? He had to because if she had to face another trip to town without his ring on her finger...in other words as a respectable married woman, she couldn't face the snide expressions and cutting remarks of the town folk.

"Otherwise what?" His dark gaze didn't waver, as if daring her to say "no" to his proposal.

"We'd never be happy. I would pine after what you wouldn't give me. Yourself and your children."

"And why are you so set on having a family?"

"I want children to love so I can give them the kind of love I never had. Growing up, I was a silly nuisance to my pa and a tool for my mother to manipulate. I want—no, I need to know—you love me and want to share your life with me and everything that goes with it." She blinked back the tears.

He sucked in a deep breath then put his arms around her and held her tight, his breath warm on her neck. When he spoke, the words came in ragged gasps. "You are the only woman I ever wanted...but losing Annie and our baby nearly sucked the life right out of me. I was as good a husband to her as I could be, and I hope I never made her feel like she was my second choice. But she was. Even so, I was happy about the baby. Then both of them lost in the space of an afternoon."

His face contorted as he blinked back the tears shining in his eyes. The muscles in his throat worked as if the words were too difficult to utter. "She shouldn't have been in the bank that day. I sent her to open up an account for the baby. It was stupid of me—I know that now—I pushed her to show more initiative. Didn't want her to be so dependent on me. My line of work, you never know what'll happen. Anyhow, it was my fault she was there."

"It wasn't your fault. You couldn't have known something would happen."

He shook his head. "But there were rumors your brother and his gang were in the area. I should've took better care of her."

"How about if I promise to stay away from the bank, the post office and the pathetic newspaper office too if you'll— now, dang it, Cordero Tate. All I want is what any woman wants. I want you in my bed every night to keep me warm and loved. And if we're blessed by children then even better."

His expression softened, he nodded ever so slightly. "You don't give me much choice. All right. I'll marry you."

"You already asked me," she said with a giggle. "I'm the one supposed to say yes."

"So you're saying you will?" His dark eyes shone full of warmth in the lamplight.

She threw her arms around his neck. "Yes!" Her heart beat so fast it fairly flew. Finally he was truly hers to love and hold dear for the rest of her days.

"Woman, you know I can't live without you. It's official. We're engaged."

"Now you don't have to," she murmured softly and pressed her breasts against his chest. He pressed his mouth to hers and kissed her hard and demanding as his tongue invaded her mouth and mimicked the in and out of lovemaking, while his cock jammed hard against her belly. Her skin grew hot and tingled with anticipation of what would come next.

He stood, pulled her to her feet and held her fast against his hard body. Her knees weakened and a curl of desire built and wove through her entire body. "I've missed your loving so much."

"Hasn't been that long—just yesterday." His breath came in ragged gasps.

"Seems like a week." Her own breathing was tortured, her breasts rising and falling with each intake of air. "I'll marry you, but I won't stop begging you to have children. But right now, I just want you to make love to me. Anyway you want. Do anything. I'm yours."

"Anything?" He chuckled and his dark brown eyes glittered with passion.

"Anything."

"I've a mind to teach you how to make love to me."

"Yes," she hissed. "I want to pleasure you. I want you to come and come like I do when you do so many wonderful things to me."

He gathered her in his arms and sped upstairs. He set her down, but when she started to undress, he shook his head. "Wait. Not yet."

In record time he kicked off his boots and stripped down naked. She reached for him, wanting to touch his trail-hardened body and claim it for her own. "No. Not yet."

"Why? I don't understand. I want to pleasure you and you won't even let me touch you."

"You think I don't get pleasure just looking at you?"

"But I'm—" She shook her head. Honestly the man had her more confused than ever.

He grinned then sprawled on her bed, levered on one elbow, his Johnson, swollen and standing at attention. More than anything she wanted to crawl in his arms and touch him. The sight of his long, lean and muscular body and the thick cock that emerged from a black patch of curls where his thighs joined sent a jolt of need to her very core.

"Undress for me," he said. "Slowly."

"Let me make sure I understand. You just want to watch me undress?"

"For now." A smiled played across his face. "You said you'd do anything."

"I did." She smiled back. Okay, if he wanted a show, she'd give him one. He'd seen it all anyway.

Slowly she unbuttoned her shirtwaist, slipped it off her shoulders and dropped it to the floor. She started to unlace the bustier, but he held up his hand. "No, the skirt first, and then the booster thing."

Unfastening the full skirt at the waist, she let it puddle around her ankles, leaving her wearing only knickers and bustier.

"Beautiful." He grabbed his cock in his fist and began moving it back and forth from the base to the head. "I pleasure myself like this when I don't have anyone else. Ever pleasure yourself? Do you know how?"

Her face heated until it burned. How had he known? She swallowed.

"Tell me. How do you give yourself pleasure?"

"Just since we've been—you know—making love. I figured out how to do it."

"Good."

His hand kept moving slowly, almost mesmerizing her.

She couldn't keep her eyes off it.

"Was it good when you did?"

She nodded. "But it's better with your mouth on me."

"Take off the corset."

His voice was husky and deep and the sound of it sent a thrill to her core. The crotch of her knickers grew damp with her arousal. She loosened the bustier ties, opened the front, exposing her breasts to his view. Cupping them, she toyed with her nipples until they budded into small firm beads.

Cord groaned and increased the speed of his fist. "Take off your bloomers."

Taking her time she complied, easing them over her hips and down her legs. Of its own accord her hand went to her cleft and began to rub her pleasure nub.

"Lie down beside me, but don't stop. I want to watch you play with your pussy."

He wanted to watch while she touched herself...down there? "Uh—"

"You said 'anything'."

She put one knee on the bed and then the other and stretched out beside him. "And I mean to keep my word." Fingering her nubbin, she squeezed her legs together.

"No. Spread 'em. I want to see your pussy while you do it." She began to lose herself in the sensations of his heated gaze on her, so close but not touching her. As if it were his hand pleasuring her and not her own. With her other hand she caressed one of her breasts and pulled at the nipple. Her body grew heated, and she moaned as the waves of pleasure took her over the brink, her thighs jittering with the release.

"Beautiful. Beautiful when you come." He groaned and fisted his cock even faster.

She rolled on her side to watch. His face was flushed as

he strained and came, spurting his seed in quick jets. As his body went limp, but not his cock, she smiled. "So that's how you pleasure yourself."

"Yeah. And you can pleasure me that way, too." Propped back up on his elbow, he grinned down at her.

Always eager to learn more, she asked, "With my fist or like you did—you know—with your

mouth?" She gave him a catlike smile. "I'd like to try it."

"Both."

"What about your seed? I mean if my mouth is on you..."

"Spit or swallow—your choice. I have it on good authority it doesn't taste bad."

"Where did you learn—no, never mind, I don't want to know."

"Darlin', a man has needs, and I'm a man, so..."

"I said never mind." She held her hands up and waved them. "I don't really want to know." Of course he'd had a wife and it'd been two years since she passed. Of course, there were those women, the soiled doves, who sold themselves at the Gold Dust. But were they called soiled for a reason?

"Don't you be thinking I've messed around with any of the girls at the Gold Dust, 'cause I haven't."

"I said I don't want to know." If not any of them then who?

"Just once, Annie...to please me."

"She loved you." If even the shy Annie could take his cock in her mouth... Star certainly could and would.

"Yes, she did."

"I love you, Cord. I always have. And I will do anything to please you."

She reached for his cock, but he stopped her and took her fingers in his mouth and sucked, licking each one.

"They taste like you. Like my woman. My love."

"Then let me taste you. Let me take you in my mouth."

He uttered a low groan then hissed, "Yes."

She grasped his semi-rigid cock and licked the tip. Slightly salty and male. His cock stirred to life under her tongue, and she opened her mouth wide to take him inside. Swirling her tongue around the head, she began to move her head up and down, sucking as she did.

His thighs quivered and he gasped, "Faster, darlin'." She obliged, hoping she was doing it right and, from her observations, she was.

His body tensed. And he came in her mouth. She swallowed the barely salty fluid. Eyes wide, she asked, "Was it good? Or at least all right?"

"God, yes." He pulled her into his arms and placed tiny kisses up and down her neck until she thought she might come again. "You're a hell of a woman, Starlight Tyler. A hell of a woman. And a hell of a woman deserves a reward."

She gave him an encouraging grin. "Surely you're not going to give me the one thing I want?" Oh, please...

He chuckled and shook his head. "No, but I am going to..." He positioned himself between her legs and buried his face in her cleft and took both breasts in his hands and pulled at the nipples. Licking and sucking her pleasure nub, never letting up, he brought her to a shuddering climax.

Drained and exhausted, she lay beside Cord, curled in his warm embrace. There was only one thing that could possibly make this night any better and he wouldn't give it to her: himself without reservation.

She caressed his cheek lovingly. "I love you so much. We have the rest of our lives to do the other."

He stiffened, turned his head and rolled away from her. "Don't spoil everything. You know why I can't."

A burst of anger flashed through her. She sat up. "Not can't. Won't." More than anything she wanted to pound her fists on his chest...anything to make him see reason. "Do you seriously believe we'll marry, set up house, go to bed each night for the next forty years and not ever make love? Really make love?"

"Woman!" He let out a groan and swung his legs over the side of the bed. "You are wearing me to distraction."

In an attempt to placate him, she gently placed her hand on his shoulder. "Look I understand about your loss, but I just can't imagine... Any other man would need—"

"Would what?" He whirled to face, anger clearly written across his face. "You're a woman with a woman's needs. What do you know about what a man would or wouldn't do? As for my needs, whether I planned it or not, come hell or high water, you're going to be my wife. I'm gonna love you and protect you. Believe I've already proved I can. And part of protecting you is not planting a baby in your womb every year until you're plum worn out from carrying. Isn't that enough?"

Star swallowed the lump in her throat and said in her meekest manner, "I guess it'll have to be." *Not by a long shot, Cordero Tate.*

Settling wasn't her strong point, but short of hog-tying him and forcing herself on him, settling was what she'd do.

For now.

Chapter Seven

Thursday morning the sun rose long before Star managed to drag herself from the bed. Never had she felt so loved in all her life, but still something was missing. In spite of the new way he'd taught her to pleasure him, he hadn't given of himself, not fully. And she wouldn't feel his love completely until he did.

It might take time, but he would love her the way she wanted and desperately needed.

Sitting on the side of the bed, she stretched and yawned then flopped back on the feather mattress.

Never wanted to get up. While her pa was gone, she answered to no one. Well, not quite no one. There was her mare, as well as another saddle horse, to feed and the chickens.

Dang it. She sat up straight. There was a wedding dress to finish. Yesterday, Selma had helped her with the bodice and the insetting of the sleeves. All Star had to do was gather up the skirt and attach it to a waistband and hem it, which would take forever because of the fullness. The bodice still needed the delicate French lace added and some detail work with the tiny pearl buttons down the front. Fortunately, Selma promised she'd return Saturday morning for a final fitting.

In spite of their disagreement last night, Cord swore he'd be back again for another lesson in the ways of love, so there was a supper to cook just in case he was early enough for that. Too bad fried chicken, green beans and potatoes were the height of her cooking skills.

Her day passed quickly enough as long as she didn't stop to think about Cord's loving lips and skillful hands. And his stubborn heart—no, she wouldn't stop to think about that either. By the time she stopped working on the dress, the skirt was gathered and half hemmed.

Hoping he would make it for supper, she warmed up the leftovers and waited.

And waited.

Disappointment and doubt descended on her. Well, he didn't exactly swear on the Bible. Something important must've required his attention. More important than seeing her and making such sweet love?

Maybe he was still put out after last night. Maybe he wasn't coming at all.

She lit the kerosene lamp and tried sewing. Finally, rubbing her eyes, she stopped. What the heck, she ought to at least try on the skirt and double-check the hemline. She shimmied out of her denims and let them fall to the floor then pulled the pale green skirt over her head and settled it around her waist.

Leaning forward, she checked where the hem fell. Perfect. Elation buzzed through her. She twirled around and squealed. Three more days and she'd be wed.

And safe.

"Looks mighty good. Didn't know my future wife had such a fine hand with a needle."

She whirled at the sound of Cord's voice. "What are you

doing there? You should give a girl some warning. Don't you know it's bad luck for you to see my wedding dress?"

"But— All right. All right. I'm hiding my eyes." He covered his eyes and turned around. "I thought you'd be happy to see me. Guess I was wrong," he teased. "Besides, that's only a half a dress, so it doesn't count. Not that I know all that much about wedding dresses and all that superstitious nonsense."

She stepped from the skirt, bundled it up in her arms and thrust it into a nearby trunk. "Now. You can turn around.

"You're sure me seeing you in your bloomers won't jinx the big day?"

"Silly." She glanced down then snatched up her trousers and tossed them on the rocker. "Have you eaten? I waited, but then I gave up on you. Anyway, there're some leftovers in the ice box."

"Sorry." He shook his head. "Had a lead on some cattle rustlers coming over the county line. Went to check 'em out. Turned out ten head had strayed and gotten lost in an arroyo."

He reached down, picked her up and carried her upstairs. "Big old waste of time when I'd rather be here with you."

"Considering how much I have to learn, I'm surely glad you found those silly cattle and found time to come all the way out here."

He set her on her feet, but she kept her arms around his neck. He unbuttoned her shirt and exposed her breasts. He eased her back on the bed and buried his nose in the valley between her breasts. "Woman, you sure smell good. Where's that fancy thing you were wearing last time?" he growled deep in his chest. "Sorta liked all that lacy nonsense."

"I'll have you know I was very busy today. Eggs to gather, chickens to feed. I'm the only one here or haven't you noticed?"

"Believe me, darlin', I've noticed." His hand dipped into her knickers and found her cleft. She squirmed under his touch as his finger slid in and out of her pussy. "Notice something else, too. You're already creaming for me."

"Take 'em off me." Heat suffused her entire body. Dammit. He was still fully dressed. She fumbled with his belt then the buttons of his trousers. "Get naked. I want to see every inch of you. Want to feel every part of you."

"Happy to oblige, darlin'." He rolled to his feet, shrugged out of his shirt, shucked his duckins and quickly toed off his boots. Standing before her was the most glorious man she'd ever seen. Those statues of naked gods in the Boston museum had nothing on Cord. Gracious. The tiny little cocks on the ancient sculptures weren't worthy of the name.

He lay down beside her and kissed her neck and nibbled on her ear. Chill bumps popped up all over her body. "Love me, Cord. Really love me. The way I want you to. It's only three more days until we wed, and I need to feel you come inside me. I want to make you happy and be a good wife."

"A good wife wouldn't be so demanding. She'd accept her man knew what was best for her. She'd understand he was trying to protect her. Do you think it's easy for me? I want to sink inside you so deep and never be parted from your sweet body again as long as I live."

"Then you'll have to punish me, because I can't be a good wife. I just know what my body and my heart want. I want what you want."

He gave a rumble of a laugh. "Punish you I will." He rolled her over on her stomach and held his hand high, but instead of spanking her, he brought his hand down and caressed her butt, kneading it then slipped two fingers into her pussy.

"Oh." Her muscles twitched. This was new. What was he up to this time?

He eased his hand toward her rear again and parted her cheeks.

Her eyes widened as he leaned over and nipped the cheek of her ass then inserted a finger into her back entrance. She pushed up on her elbows. "I think you're in the wrong—"

"Not at all. Just relax. You wanted me to fuck you and I will. Just can't do it the usual way. Get on your knees, keep your ass in the air."

He was going to fuck her. Okay, she was more than ready for that. She leaned down on her forearms and, butt in the air, she asked, "You sure about this?"

"I'll stop anytime you tell me to." With one hand, he was already rubbing the head of his Johnson up and down her pussy then up higher. With his other hand, he reached for her breast and tweaked the nipple.

The sensation was unbelievably sensual and unexpected.

She heard him spit in his hand, looked over her shoulder and saw him rubbing the moisture on his Johnson. Then he began to nudge his cock into her rear passage. She arched backward and groaned, and the head of his cock slid inside her body. She tensed. Couldn't help it.

"Take a deep breath. Relax." Giving her body time to adjust, he moved deeper into her canal then slowly pulled back. "You okay?"

She nodded then moved with him. He reached for her nub and massaged it as he thrust in and out. She met him stroke for stroke, her body burning all over. His pace increased until he was gasping along with her. Perspiration, both his and hers, mingled. Her back and his belly slapped together like wet bursts of applause.

"Can't hold any longer." He shoved into her one last time and cried out.

The pulsations of his cock, so deep within her body, sent wave after wave of heat and took her over the edge. Beneath him she collapsed and trembled while her pussy throbbed like a drummer's call to war.

He pulled out, and she rolled over on her back and cast a lazy gaze at him. He lay beside her, his head resting on his hand, his eyes half closed. "That was sure different. What do you do for an encore?"

He grinned then left her bed and walked over to the wash basin. Over his shoulder he laughed. "An encore? That was the encore, missy." He began bathing his Johnson.

"But—"

"No buttocks about it. That's all there is tonight." He reached for a rag and dampened the end of it then walked back over to the bed. "Turn over."

"You want to do that again?" As good as it felt, she sure as hell wasn't ready for another go.

"Just turn over and quit smarting off. Surely you trust me to wipe your bottom. Seems to me you're the dainty type, even if you carry on like a wh—"

"Like a whore? Is that what you think I am?"

"No, but you sure do a fine imitation." He shook his shaggy head. "Didn't know regular women..."

His words faded away as he stroked her bottom, gently cleansing her.

"Not sure I care for the comparison." Still, his tender ministrations to her backside were putting her in the mood for more loving—of the more conventional kind.

He used the other end of the towel, dried her then caressed the curves of her hips and finished by giving her a light tap full on the butt.

"So, that—what we just did—won't make me pregnant either?"

"Not unless Tyler women are made different from other women. Babes aren't in the habit of coming out that passageway."

He set a knee on the bed then lay down beside her. "Darlin', you're unlike any woman I've ever known. You seem to enjoy all the things we've done as much as I have."

"What's not to enjoy?" She levered up on an elbow to face him. "Didn't—you know—your first wife—" She broke off embarrassed to ask him. "None of my business. I'm sorry."

She watched him heave a sigh and shake his head. "Annie—she was loving, but gentle and shy. Not—"

"Not like me." She turned away. "Sorry, I had no right."

He rested his hand on her shoulder and rolled her back to face him. "It's only natural you'd want to know."

"Will you stay the night? I get so lonesome here all by myself. Almost wish Pa and the hands would hurry up and get back from Abilene."

"Not so sure I want to run into your pa before the wedding. Just as soon have that a done deal when he comes home."

"You're the sheriff. Why would you be afraid of him?"

"Man has a temper and a keen eye. Wouldn't do for him to roll in and find me here."

"The earliest they'll be home is tomorrow, midday or later. You could get up at sunrise, and no one would ever know the difference."

He rubbed his chin. "I'm giving your offer some serious thought."

She insinuated her leg between his strong thighs and scooted closer. "I wish you would. Surely you have something else to teach me?" She cupped one of her breasts and offered it to him. He groaned and positioned himself over her, latched on, kissing, sucking and grazing the taut nipple, while he slipped two fingers into her core and a third finger up her ass and started moving. Her walls gripped his fingers.

"Touch me," he gasped.

"I want you inside me. All of you."

"No. Touch me."

Reading the desperation in his tone, she grasped his swollen cock, circled it then slid her hand up and down his length rapidly as he'd shown her only the night before. Together they moved and came in a shuddering climax as one.

As he murmured sweet words in her ear, she snuggled into his arms, secure in his presence and his love.

Chapter Eight

Star gazed at her reflection in the looking glass then gave a pat to her hair. Not bad for having to do it herself. Ma had a way with hair, but she wasn't here. And it was a good thing she wasn't because she'd be having a fit over what Star was about to do.

Only two more days until she and Cord were wed. This afternoon he'd sent word by his brother Nash he'd see her again tonight. What new way to make love would he teach her this time?

Or would he finally give in and truly make love to her? Not that she didn't enjoy all the other methods he had of pleasuring her and himself—she did mightily. But it just seemed as if something wasn't right if he couldn't find it in his heart to make love to her the way men and women had made love all through time.

Is that why he left in the early morning hours without waking her?

She stopped. Listened. The sound of agitated horses nickering and stamping their feet reached her ears. What now? She'd fed the two horses, her mare Dolly and the other saddle horse, earlier. Still, better check.

She set the brush on the small oak dressing table and headed downstairs.

*

She emerged from the stables. The horses had quieted down and nothing else was out of place. As many nights as she'd spent alone on the ranch, she'd never been afraid. Still, she'd be glad when Cord came to say good night.

In the distance a coyote howled, and a shiver slid up her spine. She folded her arms across her chest and rubbed her arms. Something just didn't feel right. The bright prickles of stars couldn't make up for the fact there was no moon tonight. Only the dim light from the kerosene lamp in the kitchen provided the barest bit of illumination. Most of the area between the barn and the house was in complete shadow.

A rush of feet. She started to turn, but then a hand was clapped over her mouth. "Mm-uh!"

"Quiet or I'll slit your fucking throat."

A pair of very strong arms crushed her to his body. She fought, swinging her elbows into his ribs and kicked back at his knees.

No good.

A second pair of hands grabbed her wrists and tied them with what felt like rope. The hand over her mouth was removed, but before she could scream, something—a kerchief, most likely—was stuffed into her mouth, gagging her almost to the point where she couldn't breathe.

She kicked forward and back.

"Tie her fucking feet, before she breaks one of my legs and runs off." The second voice was guttural, but oh-so-familiar.

Her half-brother, Tom.

"Mm-unh!" What the devil was he playing at? Why treat her like this? She'd never done anything to him, unless you counted being born into the most miserable family in the entire state of Texas.

"Her horse is in the stable," her brother said. "Throw her across it. We can lead the mare as we go."

Entirely too quickly Dolly was led from the barn, already saddled, and the two men picked her up and slung her over the mare's back like a sack of feed. Her head hanging down left her so dizzy she wanted to pass out, but she was too damn mad.

Oh, just give her a chance and she'd get even.

She strained to hear what they were saying. What was her brother's demented plan?

Kidnap and ransom? Would Cord pay to get her back? What if he was glad she was gone and out of his hair?

"Appreciate the help. Won't forget it," Tom said.

"Hold on now. You said there's a reward in this for me." Again the unfamiliar voice, probably one of her brother's gang.

Reward? Maybe Teddy Darwin died from that measly little knife wound. Granted it was rather close to his shriveled manhood.

"Don't have a mind to split it."

"Fifty-fifty—that's what you said." Tension tightened the partner's tone as he insisted.

"I reconsidered."

Not good. Tom was tricky and not to be trusted on a good day. Surely his partner had enough sense not to challenge him.

"B-but you said enough for us to clear out and start new lives if we want."

Ah, stuttering. The partner was starting to panic. Maybe she should, too.

"Been thinking. I can have a better life with *all* of it."

Then a grunt. "You sumbitch. You gutted me." A muffled thud.

Silence.

Her mare whinnied then pranced in an uneasy side-step or two. She tried a soothing croon, hoping to settle her mount.

Next she heard her brother grunt and the sounds of something—his henchman?—being dragged away.

Disbelief and now fear set her heart to pounding. Her brother just killed a man. What would he do to her? Would he really slit her throat like he threatened?

Not until he collected his reward.

"Gotta head on outta here." He walked past her and snatched up the mare's reins then mounted his horse. "Places to be. Folks to see."

Didn't make sense her brother would turn her over to the authorities, since he was on the run himself. Had to be her mother or Darwin. Had they already followed her here to Texas?

Without much more than a warning, "Hyah!" the horses took off at a rapid clip. Her body jostled and slid about. Fearing she would be flung from the horse's back, she pressed her elbows into the horse's flank on one side and her knees into the opposite, hugging as tight as she could.

How far would she have to hang on like this?

Though Cord knew the trail to the Tyler ranch by heart, he kept a firm grip on the reins, and picked the way down the hill and into the valley leading to the spread. The night was a rare dark one. No point in injuring a good horse in a headlong rush to get laid.

Nights turning cooler, too. Before long it'd be fall.

He was later than he said he'd be. Hopefully she'd still wait up for him. As anxious as she was for lovemaking, she probably was. First, he'd had to settle a dispute between two drunks in town. Both now resided in his jail with Nash pulling guard duty overnight.

He shook his head. Star's coming back to Kenton Valley was more than he deserved. Yes, he'd loved his wife Annie, but not like he'd loved Star. Annie was a good wife. But maybe he'd been half-hearted in the way he loved her. No doubt she'd been a maiden true.

But loving Star was akin to being an opium eater. He couldn't get enough of her. And she seemed to feel the same way. Or maybe she just wanted to get away from her drunkard father.

Couldn't blame her for that.

In two days they'd be hitched good and proper. In two days she'd expect him to be a real husband and love her the way a man should.

How could he risk her life for his own selfish needs? The west was hard on women. Birthing was hard, too. And being shot in a holdup was totally unexpected. Could he risk losing another wife and child?

But he couldn't imagine the rest of his life without Star in his bed.

After being shot, Annie went into early labor and suffered for four long days. Her screams tore out his heart, until the end when they grew faint and fainter. Unable to stand it any longer, he pushed aside the sad-faced women who attended her laying-in to hold Annie's hand at the end.

So far gone, she didn't recognize him or even know he was there. Her poor face was ashen and clammy with sweat. The baby they finally pulled from her was pale and limp.

He held the tiny mite; tears streamed down his checks. Her hair was wild and black like his. If she'd lived, she'd have been a beauty.

Could he put Star through something like that? Could

he stand to lose another woman he loved? Especially the love of his life?

No, he couldn't. Wouldn't ever make love to her that way.

Before he knew it, he was at the Tyler ranch. His heart kicked up at the thought of seeing her again. No matter how much she begged him, he wouldn't give in to her demands. Still, she was an enthusiastic lover, this love of his life.

He brought his horse to a halt and dismounted, looped the reins at the hitching post. Brushing off the trail dust from his trousers, he strode up the steps and knocked on the door.

And waited.

He knocked again.

Maybe she'd gone to sleep. He tried the latch. It opened easily. "Star?"

Maybe she was already upstairs waiting for him. He bounded up the stairs and tapped on her door. "Star? It's me."

Dang it. She was playing some game with him. He opened the door, but her bed wasn't disturbed. A sense of unease collected on the back of his neck and sent a shudder through his body. He quickly checked the other two rooms on the second story then ran downstairs.

He headed to the kitchen where he found a kerosene lamp, burning low and smoking. The back door was standing open. Maybe she was out in the barn.

He ran to the barn, but she wasn't there and neither was her mare.

Where the hell could she have gone this time of night...in the dark?

Then he noticed it. The metallic copper smell of it. Blood.

His heart slammed in his chest and he could barely breathe.

If someone...anyone...

He followed the scent until it grew stronger. He stumbled across a body. He crouched down and ran his hands over it. Felt of the head and bearded face...a man's.

Thank God.

Relief shot through him in a rush of emotion. Weak as a newborn babe, he sank back against the wall of the barn.

Had someone attacked her? Had she gone for help?

No, he would've met her on the trail.

Dang it. Why tonight with no moon? He couldn't tell much except the dead man had been gutted.

Focus.

Wouldn't be able to see well enough to trail her until daylight. Better go back to town, assemble a search party and be ready to ride at first light.

Chapter Nine

After what seemed like hours, they stopped. Her half-brother yanked Star off the mare and threw her on the ground. The rocky terrain cut into her back and tore at her arms. With what little breath she had left, she groaned.

"Shut up, you whiney bitch." He loomed over her and yanked the gag from her mouth.

Finally.

Able to breathe freely, she gasped for air. "What the hell are you up to, Tommy Tyler?"

He flashed his usual shit-eating grin. "Got to make a living somehow."

"Heaven forbid you should run the ranch. Our drunken pa doesn't seem to give a hang about it anymore. If Ben Davis weren't such a good foreman, there wouldn't be a ranch to run." She struggled against the ropes binding her. Somehow she had to get loose before whatever he planned took place.

"Don't like cow-poking all that much. Not very rewarding."

Her bladder about to burst, she struggled more. "Untie me. I have to use the facilities."

He laughed, a raw, empty sound echoing through the dark Texas night. As far as she could see, the land was flat, and the night sky was as wide as it was dark with no sign of the moon. The ride hadn't been as long as it seemed. There wasn't a hint of daybreak yet.

He got down in her face. She caught a whiff of his whiskey breath. "Facilities? Honey, you're in Texas. Ain't no facilities or outhouses for near on twenty miles."

"You know you can't get away with this."

He let out a bark of laughter and hooked his thumbs in his braces as if he'd accomplished something noteworthy. "'Pears to me I already have."

"Cord's coming after me and he'll find us. And now you'll hang, for sure."

He pulled a flask from his hip pocket and took a long swig then wiped his mouth with his shirtsleeve. "You need to shut up before I shove this gag back in your mouth. Why'd you have to come back anyhow?"

"I didn't care for Boston." And certainly not my mother's choice of a husband.

A cagey expression crossed his face then twisted into a mask of mockery. "Bet you got yourself in trouble. Always knew you were a whore at heart like your stuck-up ma."

"No, I didn't get into trouble. Moving to Boston wasn't my idea. When I got the chance, I ran away. That's all there is to it."

"Bet your whore of a mother is looking for ya." He sniggered. "In fact, I'd bet money on it." He hunkered down and grinned. "Pa says you're still mooning over Cord."

"When did you talk to him? I haven't seen you around since I came home."

"Been around...on the quiet."

"Looking for another bank to rob? Another woman and baby to kill?"

"Tate's the sheriff. He would say something like that. Bastard." He hawked up a glob of spittle. It landed next to her boot. She drew her foot away.

"Cord's honest, and he's a good man. You used to be friends."

"Was 'til he stole my woman."

"Guess she had better sense than to marry someone like you."

Without a warning word or even a change in expression, he reached out and backhanded her.

The blow jarred her, but more than hurting, it made her mad. "I always loved him. And now I'm going to marry him." Let her brother chew on that.

"You cain't marry Cord Tate. Case you forgot, the sheriff wants to hang my ass."

"Like you don't deserve it." Stall for time. Cord would come looking for her. He had to. "If you stick around here, that's exactly what's going to happen, whether I marry him or not." She struggled against the ropes and shook her head. "As miserable a creature as you are, we grew up together—brother and sister. I don't want to see you hang. Why don't you leave Texas? Go to Canada or Alaska. Cord certainly won't be trying to find you up there. Change your name, and while you're at it, your way of living."

"My way of living? You're one to talk. Letting him use you like a fifty cent whore."

"What do you mean? How do you know—?"

"Told ya. I been around on the quiet. You were too busy to know I was in the house. But I saw him sticking his prick in your—"

"Never mind what you saw!"

"Guess you liked it a lot. You was begging for more."

God, he watched them making love? Her face burned, but she wasn't about to let her brother get away with anything. "We're getting married day after tomorrow. Besides, he can use me anyway he likes long as it doesn't hurt." She spat on the ground. "What's it to you anyway? What goes on between a man and his wife is their business."

"Boston turned you into a whore. Was that your ma's plan all along? What happened? She sell you to the highest bidder?"

"Pretty much, only..."

"What?"

"Nothing." No sense in telling her crazy, stupid brother about her mother's plan. Too humiliating. Besides she wouldn't put it past her brother to try and cash in on it by telling Theodore Darwin where she was...if he hadn't already.

If he wasn't taking her to Darwin or her mother then where?

He rose to his feet, leered then unbuttoned his pants and pulled out his Johnson.

Her heart stuttered in her chest. "No, you can't," she pleaded, hating that she whined. "I'm still your sister."

"Think I want to have a go at you? No way. Just gotta piss, that's all." He laughed. "Excuse me. I need the fas-silly-tees, too." Each syllable broadened and exaggerated with his raucous laughter.

As fast as she could, she inched back painfully and tucked her feet under her to avoid their getting wet. "Sonofabitch! Turn around at least!"

"You weren't too proud to see the high-and-mighty sheriff's prick. Figure seeing mine won't give you the vapors."

Instead of rising to his bait, she squeezed her eyes shut.

"Matter of fact, you did more'n look at his prick." He laughed again, more like the cackle of a coyote crossed with a setting hen.

"Shut up!" If she wasn't trussed up like a hog going to

market, she'd take great pleasure in shutting his mouth herself. When they were children, he'd seemed quite ordinary. Sure, he teased her a lot, but that was what big brothers did. But once he hit fourteen, his teasing turned mean and many times made her uncomfortable. At the time she wasn't sure why she started avoiding. She just did.

Now that she was older and a tad wiser in the ways of men, she was certain not-so-dear half-brother Tom meant her harm more than once. Luckily she'd been a clingy mama's girl and gave him little opportunity for unhealthy mischief.

"Bossy bitch! I'm calling the shots here. Ain't you figured that out yet?"

"So, what's your plan? Have you figured out how you're going to escape with your hide intact once Cord catches up with you?"

"Don't mock me! I won't have you making fun."

Her eyes still shut, his backhand across her face came hard and fast, but more expected this time. Her vision blurred. Tears stung her eyes from the bright points of pain across her cheek.

"Now keep your trap shut or I'll shut it for you."

Chapter Ten

By the dawn's first light, Cord, his two brothers and seven more well-armed men gathered at the Tyler spread, the Double Bar T. After they dismounted, he led the search party around the ranch house to the barn.

"Watch your step. It was pitch black last night. Couldn't see anything in the way of tracks. Don't know if we can pick up a trail or not, but we've gotta try."

He squatted on his heels and studied the ground between the house and barn. "She didn't ride out through the valley. I would've met her." More plains and hills out the back way, but in general the terrain was flatter. "Most likely whoever took her took her out that way."

"Sure enough. Star's mare is missing." He pointed. "That way. Two sets of hoof prints off to the northeast." Not surprising since there was a dead man and a strange horse wandering the property. He used it the night before to carry the stranger's body back to town.

"Maybe she left on her own," Bud Christy offered with a shrug. "Tyler women ain't know'd for sticking 'round."

A flash of anger burned through Cord's chest. He shook his head. "No-siree, Bud. Star and me—we have plans. Getting hitched on Sunday."

He eyed the group of men and dared any one of them to

laugh.

None did. None dared.

"Not gonna be easy. Ground's rocky," his brother Nash said with a discouraged air.

"Makes no difference." Luis, Cord's other brother, hunkered down and gazed at the faint prints then frowned. "We got to get a move on. He's got an eight hour lead."

"Mount up!" Cord and the search party headed back to the front for their horses. Worry bunched his shoulders into a knot. Somehow he had to find her. She wouldn't have run away. Not now. Not with their marriage just a day from being a fact.

Just before climbing into the saddle, he stopped and turned to his youngest brother. "Luis, you're the best tracker. You lead."

More than a little chilled from the night time temperatures dropping, Star shivered, unable to feign sleeping any longer. Her back muscles ached. If fact, her entire body ached from lying on the ground all night.

"Get up!" Tom kicked her thigh, more of a nudge than a true kick.

"I can't. You have to help me." If her bastard brother would just get close enough she'd kick his *cojones* clear up to his throat.

"I'll help you all right." He kicked her again with the toe of his boot.

Bastard. A sharp pain shot though her upper thigh. She winced and glared at him with her best let-me-get-free-and-see-what-I'll-do expression then gave up and rolled over to her knees and eased to her feet, struggling a bit to regain her balance. "Where're you taking me?"

"You'll see soon enough." He grabbed her roughly, ready

to throw her body over the saddle.

Think. "Just let me ride upright and tie my hands in front of me. It's all I'll be able to do to keep in the saddle."

"Can't take a chance on you gettin' away. You're worth too much."

A shiver of fear speared its way through her. "Worth too much? I'm not the one with a bounty on my head."

"You'd be surprised." He let out a grating laugh.

Somehow she had to get away before he got her on the horse. She jammed her knee into his gut. With a grunt, he dropped her. She landed on her feet and took off in a dead run.

Dammit. Nothing but plains and hills as far as she could see. If she could just get far enough ahead, she could slip into one of the caves that abounded in the area.

Hell. Who was she fooling? How could she outrun a man on a horse when all she had were her two feet?

Her brother recovered quickly—too quickly—and grabbed her by the collar of her shirtwaist and shook her like a dog with a rabbit. "Not so fast." He shoved her to the ground then whipped a rope around her ankles as if she were a runaway calf.

"You just better be glad he wants you alive or the buzzards would already be circling for their dinner."

"What the hell? Where are you taking me?"

"Shut your trap." He threw her across her mare and tied the reins to his pommel. "Let's just see you try to get away now."

Only one person could be behind the reward offer. Teddy Darwin. Had he followed her all the way to Texas? Or was it one of those damned Pinkerton agents he was so fond of hiring?

Teddy she could manage...provided she could just get loose.

*

The sun grew high overhead, and although Tom stopped and watered the horses, he didn't offer her so much as a sip from his canteen.

"You bastard. I'm dying of thirst. If I'm dead you won't get your reward. Isn't that right?"

"Just shut up. Ain't all that far. Another day's ride."

"I can't go that long without water!" But he just kept riding and ignoring her. If she could just see where he was taking her. But no, she'd lost her bearings. It seemed like he'd circled around some. So maybe she wasn't as far from home as she thought.

In the distance she heard the clatter of a train. They were close to the tracks. Maybe ten miles or so from the ranch.

Or twenty.

Time passed so slowly. The ground, for that was all she could see, grew rockier, and their progress had slowed. She was no longer jostled around like a sack of feed corn. Shadows lengthened, and the sun had passed its zenith. Hunger and thirst were bad, but hanging with her head down for hours had left her dizzy and confused.

If he would just stop somewhere.

Anywhere.

Then finally some shade, more shadows. He was leading her through an opening between high steep boulders then to a cave entrance. His old hideout near the San Saba mines?

The horses slowed then stopped.

"Took you long enough to reach this godforsaken place." The sound of a new voice reached her.

An unfamiliar one. One without a Texan drawl.

"Alive and kickin' just like you ordered. Mighty tempted to bring her otherwise, though."

"That wouldn't have been wise." The newcomer's voice was educated and matter of fact.

Even dizzy and confused, she didn't miss the ominous threat underlying his tone. It certainly wasn't old Teddy Darwin. No, his patrician lisp was only too familiar.

"Why would you treat your sister in such a manner?" the stranger asked.

"She's feisty. 'Fraid she'd get away from me."

Two strong arms grabbed her and pulled her from the back of her mare and set her on her feet.

A wave of dizziness washed through her, and she staggered. The stranger reached out and steadied her then bent down and untied her feet. She leaned against his shoulders to keep her balance. The acrid smoke of a small cigarillo reached her nose.

"Water," she gasped. "Thirsty." The words came out in a croak.

Her vision cleared a bit, in time for her to see him glare at her brother.

The stranger threw down his cigarillo and guided her over to a rock. "Sit."

"Fine." Nodding, she sat.

He ambled over to a black stallion and fetched back a canteen. "Drink." He held it for her.

She gulped the water. It was warm, but fresh enough. Water dribbled from the corner of her mouth. Turning her head, she tried to wipe her mouth on her shoulder.

"I'll loosen your bindings, if you promise not to run."

She glanced around and rolled her eyes. "Where do you think I'd go?"

His grim face relaxed for a moment. "You have a point."

He untied her hands. She rubbed them until the feeling began to return. She took some time a good look at the stranger. Tall, dressed in black from head to toe, he was handsome but grim, with angular features and pale eyes that didn't smile.

"Aw-right. I brung her. Now pay me. You can tend to all her complaints after I vamoose."

"Five hundred, I believe?"

"That's right."

"Five hundred? That's an outrage," she said. "You sold me out for five hundred dollars?"

The stranger said dryly, "Think you're worth more, do you?"

"Yes, not to mention, there's such a thing a family loyalty." She folded her arms across her breasts. "Obviously not in my family."

"Listen to the whore running her mouth about family loyalty. I don't claim kin. No, sir."

"Rest assured, young lady, you're worth quite a bit more to my employer."

"Then I want more, too," Tom shouted. His stance widened and his hand hovered in the air at the level of his gun butt.

"No. In fact, considering our deal was to deliver her in good condition, I would be within my rights to reduce your fee to half what we agreed. If you wish more, you must earn it. I suggest you accompany us to meet my employer and make your demands personally."

"I shorely will!" Her brother shook his head and strutted back and forth then nodded. "She's a feisty one. You might need some help getting her there."

The stranger shot a quick glance in her direction.

She wrinkled her nose. "Two men to handle one woman. That's rich."

"You might be correct, Tyler."

She swallowed her relief. At least the stranger wasn't intent on humiliating and mistreating her. At least, that was her first impression. Her gaze darted from side to side. That didn't mean she wouldn't still try to get away.

"You're safe with me," her new captor said.

Sheer exhaustion drained her body of energy. She trembled. If she could just make her feet move. Somehow she had to get away from both of them. "Who are you? You're a Pinkerton, aren't you?"

Narrowing his gaze, the man sat down on a rock and studied her. He tipped his hat with two fingers. "Agent Fields, at your service, ma'am."

"And you're employed by...Theodore Darwin."

Coolly, he nodded his agreement.

"You know..." She raised her chin a notch. "You're not the first he's sent after me."

"He must value you highly." His tone was dry as if he couldn't understand why anyone would value her.

"He's a lecherous old puke."

He raised a skeptical brow. "I'm to bring you to him. That's all I'm paid for. What happens afterwards is nothing to me."

"But I'm getting married on Sunday." Surely he could see she wanted no part of Teddy Darwin.

"Really?" The Pinkerton shrugged. "I have no information regarding Mr. Darwin's intentions."

"I'm not talking about marrying Teddy Darwin. I'm promised to the sheriff of Kenton Valley, and I just imagine he's already on my trail."

Fields raised his brows. "I wonder."

"Why would you say that? I'm missing and I'm definitely worth finding." Damn straight she was.

"Considering the amount of trouble you've already

caused your brother and Mr. Darwin, it's conceivable the good sheriff will give up the chase and count his lucky stars."

"Oh, no, he won't."

He laughed. "Already taken him to your bed, have you?"

"I'm expecting his baby," she lied without even a heating of her cheeks.

"Admirable." He nodded as if truly meant it. "A woman who knows how to get what she wants. Certainly didn't waste any time. Did you?"

"Told you my sister was no better than a whore...like her no-good ma."

"What a wonderful brother I have. She raised you after your ma died. You should be grateful instead of sullying her name." Why she was defending her admittedly no-good mother was a mystery, but apparently blood was thicker than water. "You do know you're dealing with a bank robber, don't you?"

Fields nodded. "That's his problem. Not mine. The reward on you is significantly higher than any bounty on his head."

Try as she might, she couldn't help but think about when they were young. There was actually a time when she loved her big brother. He'd looked out after her. He hadn't always been this bad. Maybe if she hadn't left home, he wouldn't have turned to robbing banks.

"Better get a move on," the Pinkerton said. "I'd rather not spend another night in this cave."

"Used to better lodgings are you?" She lifted her lip in a sneer. "That is, when you're not kidnapping women."

He took a step forward. "It's a job. That's all." His gaze traveled up and down her body.

She shivered and crossed her arms as if she could protect herself from his steely gaze. "Please. You seem a reasonable man. I'm promised to another."

"The story I heard is you were first promised to Mister Darwin."

"My mother promised, not me. Besides, he's old—at least forty."

"Is he now? That ancient? Miss Tyler, it's unfortunate, but I was hired to bring you unharmed to Mr. Darwin and make no mistake, I will do so."

"They say his first wife did away with herself."

Fields frowned. "You can't believe everything you hear."

She set her hands on her hips. "Right after my mother informed me we were engaged, he tried to force himself on me. Most undignified."

"And hasn't the sheriff had his way with you? Or were you lying about being with child?"

"No! I'm with child all right. I don't imagine that'll sit very well with old Teddy." She remembered to cross her hands over her lower belly like she'd seen pregnant women do.

"Don't imagine it will."

"Don't listen to the bitch." Her brother sat on a rock and started picking his teeth with a dirty fingernail. "Every word outta her trap is a lie."

Ignoring her brother's foul mouth, she grasped the front of the Pinkerton's shirt. "Please. Just take me home. My father's spread is just outside Kenton Valley."

Fields pried her fingers away one by one then stepped back. "And where's your father?"

"On a trail drive and probably drunk." Desperation seized her. "The sheriff will give you a reward for returning me."

"For bringing you back to his loving arms? Even if I were inclined to go against my employer's wishes, I doubt the reward would make it worth my while."

"But—"

"And after only a few minutes in your company, I'm of the mind your sheriff might be glad somebody took you off his hands."

"But—" Dammit, the man was fond of the sound of his voice.

"Now, if you can find it in yourself to get back on that mare, we'll be going."

She held her hand to her forehead in a limp gesture. "I-I just don't know. I'm still mighty weak."

"Her? Weak?" Tom gave a snort. "Never had a weak day in her life."

She shot a hateful glare in her brother's direction. If she could just get her hands on him, he'd be sorry he was ever born.

Another long and lazy, all too knowing glance then the Pinkerton raised a dark brow. "You're fine. At least I'll allow you to ride astride."

"As opposed to being slung over the back of the horse like a sack of feed?" She sprang to her feet, ready to fight if she had to.

"Yes, that."

"And my hands?"

Her brother gave a snort and mounted his horse. "She'll run first chance she gets."

"With two of us, that won't happen, now will it? We'll make better time if she's not bound." He turned to face her. "But then your brother doesn't trust you, and he certainly knows you better than I." One corner of his mouth lifted in a half smile. "Besides, Mr. Darwin says you're a dab hand with a knife."

"He said that, did he?" She smiled. "He's lucky I didn't geld him while I was at it. Believe me, I tried."

Fields laughed and showed his teeth, white and even.

"I'm sure you did your best."

"Laugh all you want. I told you. My betrothed is the sheriff of Los Marcos County. He *will* come after me and arrest you both."

"You might've mentioned that fact before. Besides, Mr. Darwin was your betrothed first. He has prior claim. In addition, he's paying me a handsome sum to bring you to him." He walked over to her mare and led the creature by the reins. "Mount up."

He waited for her response, but she averted her gaze and ignored him.

"Now."

"Where's he waiting? It figures he wouldn't bother to ride out into the countryside to retrieve me." Desperation gathered in her gut threatening to overwhelm her. "You have to understand—"

"Enough. Get on your horse." His words came out sharp and cutting as a whip.

"Fine." She trudged over to Dolly, stuck her boot in the stirrup, grabbed the pommel and swung a leg over the mare's back.

"Ain't it a miracle." Her brother hooted. "Looks like she's not so weak after all."

Fields loosely tied her hands together in front of her. "You can still manage the reins?"

"Yes." What did he think she was, some idiot Boston debutante who only rode in the park?

And at the first opportunity, if their attention so much as faltered, she'd take off into the hills. Now that she was pretty sure where she was.

"Don't think you're going to get away." The Pinkerton kept her horse's lead in his hand and moseyed over to his horse and tethered Dolly's lead to his saddle.

Still, she couldn't give up. Had to be some way to make

him see reason, even if her brother never would. "Your employer doesn't love me. It's a financial agreement between him and my mother."

"Makes no difference."

"What if he means me harm? You wouldn't want something like that on your conscience, would you?"

"Ma'am, you have no idea what I have on my conscience. As things go, this is minor."

"I had to defend my honor."

He leveled his gaze on her. "And yet you've already surrendered it to the sheriff. Your *honor* seems an inconvenient thing at best."

His ironic emphasis on the word honor let her know he didn't think much of her. Let him think what he would. What did she care? All she had to do was soften him up and take whatever advantage there was. "You're a man. You wouldn't understand."

He nodded. "You're right. I don't."

She clamped her jaw and bit back the heated reply burning on her lips. Damn him. And damn Cord, too. Where the hell was he anyway? Didn't he care she'd been kidnapped? Maybe he hadn't come to the ranch last night after all. What if no one knew she was missing?

A hard lump rose in her throat, and she choked back a sob. If Cord didn't find her, she was doomed to live whatever kind of life old Teddy deemed fit. She'd be nothing more than his property.

No, she wouldn't give up. Cord would know something was wrong. He would come after her. He would.

Until then, her only hope was reaching a town. Maybe then she could prevail on some kind soul to assist her. She couldn't help it. Her mouth tugged into a smile at the thought getting away from the Pinkerton and her brother.

"Don't even think it. You can't get away."

The Pinkerton's words snapped her back to reality. Schooling her responses, she gave a casual shrug.

Chapter Eleven

The sun grew lower in the western sky. Cord whipped off his hat and mopped his forehead with his kerchief. All he could think about was Star. Would he ever see her again? Twice now, she'd been taken from him. Last time he'd been too young and too stupid to follow. And her mother had taken her clear across the country.

Not this time.

Half hour ago, Luis had ridden ahead, scouting the trail. At the sound of his returning hoof beats, Cord raised his gaze. His brother...in a big hurry. "What'd you find?"

"Cave up ahead," he gasped. "Someone's been there recently. Tracks of three horses, two large sets of boot tracks and a third, smaller boot size. Could be a woman's."

Star might be fond of her cowboy boots, but her foot was on the dainty side. His heart slammed in his chest like a battering ram. "But until now, there's only been two sets of horse tracks."

"Looks like they met up with someone who smoked pricey cigars. They were all over the ground."

A sense of dread centered in his gut, threatening to loosen his bowels. "What else?"

"Another trail, three horses, heading west toward

Llano."

"Llano? What the hell's in Llano?"

"Don't know. That's just where the trail leads."

Unable to keep the biting edge from his tone, he glared up at his younger brother. "And the two of 'em have Star."

"Yeah. Been meaning to ask you 'bout that." Luis swept off his hat and wiped his face with a sleeve.

"Nothing you need to know, except this. We're getting hitched on Sunday—if we can find her."

"Got any idea why her brother'd carry her off in the first place?"

"I'll be bound has something to do with money."

One of the posse rode up and cleared his throat. "See here, Sheriff."

Cord glared at him. "What it is?"

"Some of us were talking. We've got things need doing back home. Heading to Llano wasn't part of the deal."

"Dammit. Still got a missing woman on our hands, in addition to a dead man. Whoever has Starlight Tyler is a killer. I can't force you..." He rose slowly to his feet and leveled his gaze on each man one at a time. "But I'd consider it a personal favor if you boys would give me and my brothers a hand. If you can't, we'll continue on our own."

Bud Christy had the grace to stare at the ground, but other than Cord's brothers, the rest of the posse men turned their horses and headed back to Kenton Valley.

Couldn't blame 'em. Star was his fucking problem and would be 'til death parted them...if she wasn't the death of him. Just hoped that day didn't come too soon.

"Let's head out!" Cord motioned for his brothers to follow, dug his heels into the horse's flanks and headed him northeast.

*

Tired, hungry, more than a little thirsty, Star'd had enough. Not to mention she definitely smelled worse than her horse. And that poor creature was beginning to falter, not to mention needing a good rubdown.

"Where are we going, Mr. Fields? I thought we were going to meet Darwin in town. Besides, my horse requires the services of a decent livery stable." If her sense of direction was any good at all, the small town the Pinkerton was circling had to be Llano. But the sun had set at an hour earlier, and the only visible lights were from scattered campfires on the periphery.

Her brother grumbled something low and most likely foul.

The Pinkerton looked over his shoulder. "Won't be much longer. My apologies for overtaxing your mount."

The agent and her no-good half-brother kept moving and leading her away from civilization, not that Texas cow towns were particularly civilized, not like Boston was. But at least there should be a sheriff who could...

"My employer thought it best to have this reunion outside town. He procured a residence for the occasion."

"Outside the earshot of the law you mean." She gave a huff of frustration. Somehow she had to get away before Darwin got a-hold of her. No telling what that lousy leech would do. She struggled against the ropes binding her wrists. They were rubbed raw, and earlier in the heat of the day, she'd perspired. Now they burned and stung like a whole passel of fire ants had attacked her.

If, and it was a big if, Cord was somewhere behind, surely he could follow their trail.

Damnation! She needed a bed. Her back felt like the International and Great Northern railroad had laid tracks up and down her spine, and some fiend was pounding in the stakes with every step her horse took. And even though she was accustomed to riding for long periods, the muscles in her thighs were painful. Doubtful her knees would ever meet again. Her trip from Boston to Texas had taken two months, but she'd utilized various forms of transportation besides horseback: trains, stages, even hitched a ride on a covered wagon, and none of them compared to this day-long journey into hell.

In the blue-black distance the sky was wide and never seemed to end. Pinpoints of stars were the only illumination now that Llano was behind them. "How much longer? I'm about to pass out." Whining was easier now. No need to pretend. Not that it did a damn bit of good.

"Stop your damn whining. Wish I'd taken whatever I was offered," her brother said.

"Twenty minutes," the Pinkerton said, glancing over his shoulder. "Surely you can last another twenty minutes."

She let out a groan. "You're worse than my brother ever thought about being. You're supposed to bring me in unharmed."

"Are you harmed?" He snorted. "You drank the last of my water an hour ago. I wager I'm thirstier than you."

"Not giving you any of mine, ya worthless female."

Her brother didn't so much as turn around. He was too intent on the money he would earn by turning her over to old Teddy. "And who said chivalry was dead?" she muttered under her breath, and while she was at it, damned them both to the ninth ring of Hell.

Cord and his brothers reached the outskirts of Llano long after the sun had set and long after they'd lost the trail of the three horses, one of which had to be Star's.

"Too dark. Can't see a damn thing." Luis rubbed his eyes and yawned.

"Might as well camp here." Cord dismounted. "We'll pick up their trail as soon as the sun's up, even if we have to backtrack. No telling where she is."

After caring for their horses, the three brothers each paid a visit to the town's three saloons and turned up not a dad-blamed thing. Not a single sighting of two men accompanied by a young redheaded woman on horseback.

Frustrated by their lack of success, Cord crouched in front of the campfire and chewed on a strip of jerky. "What if we've lost 'em?" He closed his eyes for a second, not wanting to believe they hadn't caught up with the three yet. "Maybe they turned off the road and headed farther north?"

Hunkered down beside Cord, Luis frowned and shook his head. "As long as it was light to see, those tracks led straight to Llano. Gotta be here. Or somewhere close by."

Nash leaned back against his saddle, his long legs stretched out in front of him. "Might as well get some shut-eye. 'Nother long day ahead."

Shoving his hat over his face, Cord gave a grunt. Sleep? Damn near impossible when all he could think about was Star's slender legs parting for his mouth, her flame-red hair spilling across a lacy pillowcase. His cock hardened with the memory. Her hunger for lessons in loving and her eagerness to pleasure him left him weak with need. No man ever had a woman like Star. Losing her again wasn't an option.

And the thought of anybody else touching her silken skin sent red hot pokers of fire to his gut.

He'd kill 'em. He would.

*

"Twenty minutes" seemed much longer, but finally Star made out two torch lights, and through an iron gate, adobe walls and the long low roofline of an old hacienda-style ranch house. A heady flower-like scent reached her nose. Night-blooming jasmine?

"Fields to see Mr. Darwin," the Pinkerton said to the cowboy who ran out to open the gates.

They rode inside, and the gates clanged shut. Were they locked or were they just for show?

Not that the Pinkerton or her brother would give her much time for planning an escape. "See these horses are cared for," Fields ordered the cowboy. "They've been ridden long and hard, especially the mare."

He dismounted and pulled Star from the mare. She staggered and fell against him. His chest was hard with muscle, but he was nothing like Cord.

And handsome as the Pinkerton agent thought he was, he couldn't hold a candle to Cord's tall, sun-kissed self or his hard body.

He yanked her forward by the wrists. "Let's go."

Oh, God. Her breathing grew ragged. No way could she face Darwin again. Stall for time. "Please, give me a minute to steady myself. I can barely walk."

"If only the journey had a similar effect on your mouth." His tone had a harsh, gravelly rasp.

Was she too proud to beg? Not at all. "Look, you don't have to take me to him. I'll double whatever he's paying you." Somewhere she'd find the money, she would.

"Considering my employer wouldn't care for that arrangement, I'll decline your pretty offer—not that I believe you have the funds to follow through."

"My betrothed will."

"That's a pile of horse shit," her brother said. "Haven't exactly seen him doggin' your trail."

"And," the Pinkerton added, "I doubt he could afford to go that high. My employer could still outbid him."

"You're lower than a sidewinder's belly, Pinkerton." She bent down to pick up some dirt to throw in his eyes. This was her last chance to get away.

"Enough!" He grabbed her wrist with one hand and twisted it behind her back. "You've steadied yourself. Inside. *Now*."

"Ow!" In spite of his no-nonsense, gruff manner, he released her wrist and assisted her up the steps to the ranch house then led her through the massive carved mesquite door.

Fields stopped and motioned her brother aside. "Tyler, wait in the foyer. I'll settle with you myself."

Her brother grumbled under his breath, but he nodded.

Uneasily she walked forward. What choice did she have? Her boots clicked on the Saltillo tile floors. The walls were over a foot thick, and at the far end of the main room, a fire burned in the fireplace, taking the chill off the night air. Kerosene lamps provided the only other illumination.

Her gaze darted around the room. Where was Darwin?

"About time you brought me my package, Fields."

Darwin's familiar voice rumbled from a dark corner. "Bring her closer," he said. "I want to see how well she fared during her arduous journey."

The agent nudged her toward the warm hearth, but there was no warmth in Darwin's tone.

"I can walk," she said, inching toward the light. She could just barely make out Darwin's form in the tall-backed Queen Anne chair.

He reached out and adjusted the lamp's wick. "Ah, yes, there you are. Such a frown on your pretty face. You should be glad I cared enough to follow you here and save you from a hard-scrabble existence in the Texas Hill Country.

And your dear mother will be very pleased to know you'll keep your part of her bargain after all." He stood and ran his hand down her cheek, a sickening smile curving his thin lips.

Unable to control herself, she flinched from his touch.

"Fields will telegraph your mother tomorrow of our immediate marriage. We already have her blessing."

"I'm not a piece of property she can sell to the highest bidder. I won't marry you tomorrow or any other day."

"It's already arranged." He smiled, but it held no warmth. "The minister will arrive at ten in the morning and you will be my lovely bride by ten-thirty."

Gathering all her anger and will, she arched her chin. "No!"

"Understand this. You will be my bride or you'll be no one's."

The thought of being his bride and what that phrase meant sickened her. "I'll run away again. I won't—"

"Hold on, Darwin." The Pinkerton stepped between her and odious Darwin. "I've fulfilled my contract. I brought her here as you requested, but I'll have no part in harming this woman."

"You may leave now."

"Not as long as there's any chance you'll hurt her. If she doesn't marry you in the morning, I'll see she gets back home."

"She *will* marry me in the morning." Darwin tone was fiercely determined as he whirled. His abrupt movement knocked a vase from a side table to the floor where it splintered on the hard tiles.

Startled by the sound and fury of his response, she stepped back. "I'm already promised to someone else—the sheriff of Los Marcos County. He'll be here by morning. There'll be no ceremony," she said, determined to never give in to Darwin's plan. Desperate to turn him away, she said, "I'm already with child by him. You might as well let me go."

Darwin's face contorted with anger. "Whore!" He spit the word at her. "Just like your mother. Spread your legs for someone else when I paid good money to have you unsullied." Fists clenched, he advanced.

The rage in his face, the tension in his body, took her aback. He meant to do her harm—maybe even kill her.

The Pinkerton stepped between them, holding Darwin back. "Not another step, Darwin."

"Y-your services are no longer required, Agent. You're discharged."

The Pinkerton's hand hovered over his Colt. "I will protect this young woman. It appears she has good reason to fear a marriage contract with the likes of you. Here's what will happen now. She'll be taken to a room and treated with respect. She's in need of a bath, and her horse is in need of feed, water and rest. Tomorrow, no matter what you will, I'll return her home to her father's ranch."

"How dare you order me in such a fashion! I've paid you good money, and you've reneged on your duty."

Her brother stepped forward. "Pay me instead. I'll see she marries you."

Darwin's eyes bugged. "Fields, who's this?"

"I'm her brother and I'm the one responsible for bringing her here. I want his cut."

The Pinkerton shrugged. "Notify my agency. They may even refund part of your fee—if you're lucky."

Star remained quiet, for once. It seemed the Pinkerton possessed slightly more conscience than she'd previously thought.

Hope rose and eddied through her. She might still make it back home...to Cord.

"I'll remain on guard through the night so she's not interfered with."

Tom stepped forward, his hand on his six-shooter.

Fields turned on her brother. "Don't try me, Tyler. I'd soon as shoot you as step on a bug."

Her brother slowly moved his hand away and stepped back. The coward.

Her heart hammered. Darwin wouldn't get his hands on her this time. Fields treated her with more consideration than her mother had. She glanced at him, afraid to speak, but hoped he knew how grateful she was.

As for Darwin, another coward, he seemed to shrink before Field's strength of purpose. He sputtered and gnashed his teeth, but he called the Mexican housekeeper and instructed her to see to Star's needs.

Fields followed and positioned himself outside her door. "Thank you," she whispered and closed the door. Would he be able to stay awake all night? He'd had as long a day as she, and she'd fall asleep as soon as her head hit the pillow.

The servant filled a copper tub with hot water and helped Star to undress. Fatigue had leached all the strength from her body. She eased slowly into the steaming tub of water and began to wash away the trail dust. The soap stung her raw wrists, but the heat felt incredibly good to the rest of her sore muscles. She relaxed against the tub where the maid had placed a rolled a towel for her neck.

While Star soaked, the servant left to fetch drinking water and something for Star to eat. She glanced over her shoulder to make certain her captor, now guardian, was in place at her door. He was. A sigh of relief escaped.

Tomorrow surely, Cord would find her. And the nightmare of the last day would be over. He would hold her in his arms and they would marry. She would have his babies and all her problems would be solved.

So what if her mother had sold her to Darwin? Star Tyler wasn't a piece of property. No indeed.

Darwin could just haul his withered backside back to Boston...

Or to Hell. It didn't matter which.

Chapter Twelve

Sunrise came early. Cord and Nash headed into town while Luis backtracked to pick up Star's trail. As soon as the general store opened, Cord went in and bought provisions to last the rest of their trip. When he paid, he used the occasion to ask the storekeeper some questions. "I'm looking for two men and a woman. Woman's pretty—a redhead. Not sure about the men, but she's been taken from her home in Kenton Valley, and I'm pretty sure it's against her will. My posse and I have followed their trail here, but nobody's seen 'em."

The storekeeper eyed Cord's badge. "No strangers in town. Now, I hear there's a Yank staying out at the governor's old ranch. Haven't seen him, nor heard about any young woman."

"How far?"

"Five miles give or take. Northeast of town. Road ain't bad, unless it's raining. Then it floods."

"It's dry now."

"Yeah, so 'tis." The storekeeper nodded.

"A Yankee you say?"

"Yeah, a highfaluting one, so they say. Come to think of it, his housekeeper came in here earlier this week. Bough t some of my French-milled soap. Don't get much call for the fancy stuff."

What the hell, it was a lead. And a slim one at that. "Describe the ranch."

"Hacienda style. Left over from the Mexicans. Gated, adobe, tile roof."

"Thanks." Cord gathered the provisions and left the store. Hope built in his chest until it nearly burst. Had someone from Boston kidnapped Star? He'd bet his saddle on it. Well, they wouldn't get away with it. She was his woman, and he wasn't about to let anyone take her without a fight.

Never again.

The sun was high in the wide Texas sky when Star awakened with a start. She sat up, groaned and lay back. Every part of her body hurt, including her hair. Another day's respite and she might, just might, be able to mount a horse again.

Maybe.

The door opened and the maid rushed in. "Hurry, *señorita*, you must get dressed. The minister's on his way to marry you to *Señor* Darwin."

Fury sparked and burst into flame. "No! The man's a pig." She looked over the housekeeper's shoulder. "Where's Mr. Fields—you know—the Pinkerton fellow?"

She shrugged. "*Señor* Darwin says he's gone."

"No. No! He can't be." Just as quickly panic doused her anger and set her to trembling. "He said he'd take me home today."

"Must have changed his mind. All I know, I supposed to have you dressed and downstairs in fifteen minutes. This is what *el jefe* say." Uncertainty pulled the woman's dark brows together, but her lips thinned to a determined, straight line.

Damn that Pinkerton. Should've known he wouldn't keep his word. Desperate, Star swung her feet to the cool tile floor and sat on the side of the bed. She grabbed the woman's hands. "Please, you have to help me get away. I'm in love with someone else. He's coming for me. I know he is."

The woman's eyes widened as if alarmed. "No can do. I know my place."

"Time... I just need a little time. Tell him I'm getting ready, but I want to be perfect for the wedding. Please... He's a horrible man. He wants to hurt me because I ran away from him before. I'm afraid..." It was partially true. He did want to hurt her. Last night, she'd seen the sick anger in his eyes and heard the disgust in his voice.

But afraid of him—no. She'd kill him before she'd let him lay another slimy finger on her.

Cord met up with his brothers on the edge of Llano and related what the shopkeeper told him about the Yank and the housekeeper's buying fine French soap.

Luis nodded. "Sounds right. I picked up their trail again. They skirted town and headed northeast." He pulled on his horse's reins and aimed the animal in that direction.

"Hold on!" Cord said. "Storekeeper said the main house is walled and gated. Property belongs to the fucking governor. We can't just go busting in there. Need a plan."

Nash shook his head in disgust. "What the fuck are we gonna do then? Just march up, show our badges and ask 'em nicely to hand her over?"

"First of all, we'll have a look-see." Cord sat straight in the saddle and tried to loosen the knotted ridges of sore muscles. "See how many guns he's got backing him. And go from there."

"Sure wish you hadn't let the rest of the posse go home," Luis said.

"Yeah. Now we know I ain't a fucking mind reader. Not that I had much choice anyway." Cord let out a good-natured chuckle. "Who knew Star'd get herself abducted, much less by someone with influence?"

Nash snorted. "Who knew you'd be this hot to trot after any woman, especially a Tyler?"

"Shut your fucking mouth before I have to hurt you. Need you too bad right now." Realizing his words were harsh, he softened his tone and added, "All you need to know is the lady and I came to an understanding. We're getting hitched."

Nash settled his hat on his head. "If we find her and if she's still willin'."

Cord couldn't help it when a wide grin tugged at his mouth. "She's willin' all right. Quit jacking your jaws. Let's find her."

Star glanced at the garments she was supposed to be married in and curled her upper lip. "I doubt this will fit."

"*El jefe* says your mama provided the measurements."

Thanks a whole hell of a lot, Mama. She'd sold her daughter off to the highest bidder like prime breeding stock to the sorriest excuse for a bull anyone ever saw.

"I can dress myself," she told the maid in her haughtiest manner, hoping the woman would leave her alone long enough for an escape. All she had to do was dart through the French windows and run to the stables, saddle her mare and race away. Not counting the gates. And the guards. Somehow she'd get through them.

The servant held up a full corset. "I lace you up."

"No, I refuse to wear one of those things. I prefer to breathe." Running away trussed up like a turkey would only slow her down.

"*El jefe*, he will not be pleased."

"That's his problem. Not mine. Now go. If you won't help me, leave me in peace long enough to gather my composure."

The woman frowned, bowed silently and withdrew.

Star glanced around the room and couldn't find the clothes she'd worn on the trail. Dammit, the wedding garments would have to do.

So be it.

She pulled the gray silk skirt over her head and settled it around her waist. Too small. Obviously her mother had given him measurements as if she were wearing a corset. She fastened the skirt as best she could, but it was at least two inches too small. No doubt the bodice would present the same problem.

So...what. She'd let it gap where it would and damn the rest. As long as half of her was covered, she didn't care what wasn't.

Her boots were gone, too Dammit! He certainly wasn't making her escape easy. She slipped into the dove gray silk wedding slippers. At least they fit.

She stepped to the door and opened it, sucked in the dry Texas air. The smell of meat cooked over an open fire reached her nose. Her stomach growled. No time for food.

She took a single step onto the shaded porch when a tall man armed with a rifle materialized from the shadows. "Sorry, ma'am. You need to go back inside."

She straightened her back. "Where's Mr. Fields? He's supposed to take me home."

The tall gunman shrugged. "Heard tell he left during the night."

could barely breathe.

The woman shoved her toward the door. "*Dios*. Go! Marry this bad man and get it over with. Get out of here. You nothing but trouble. He nothing but trouble."

If he beat the poor housekeeper, what would he do to the very person who stabbed him with a serving knife back in Boston?

Dammit, Cord. Get a move on.

With no other choice, she eased out the door. And edged toward the room where she'd seen Darwin the night before.

"Ah, there's my lovely bride." He stood attired in a dove gray morning coat and silk vest. He held an ivory-headed cane in his left hand and tapped it in the palm of his right. "The minister should be here any moment. You don't look too much the worse for wear."

"As if you cared. You beat that poor woman, just because she couldn't keep me in the room. Did you beat the man I kicked in his *cojones*? No, probably not. He's bigger than you and you only pick on those who can't fight back."

An eerie smile played about his thin lips. "Fire. I like women with fire."

"I'll show you fire." She set her hands on her hips. "Just give me a match and I'll burn down this damn place right over your head."

"I believe you would. Too bad your mother's not the hellcat you are. She was much more willing for my attentions, but once I saw you, she was a pale substitute. Only you would do."

"Shut up about my mother." Her stupid mother. How could any woman trade her daughter for a better place in society? Living with her rich brother wasn't good enough. She wanted a rich son-in-law.

"Once your precious mother saw how it was with me, she sold you as surely as a madam sells the services of one of her whores. Her price was high, and I mean to collect...payment in full." He uttered the last words with a high note of glee, as if impressed with his powers of speech.

"Last time I checked, slavery was outlawed. Illegal—you do know what the word means, don't you? I mean, you're a lawyer."

His face flushed; his mouth twisted in derision. "Don't be stupid. Deals like this have been made for centuries. You're the dowry I bought and paid for. Because of my name and fortune, you and your whore of a mother will enjoy the privileges and associate with the highest levels of Boston society, instead of existing on her brother's charity."

"I don't care about privilege and money. I'm in love. Not that you'd know what love is."

He continued as if he hadn't heard her. "Of course I can't bring you home until you're tamed." He smiled down at her, a sickening scary lurch of his lips, as if they were unused to the effort. "And how I look forward to that."

She threw back her shoulders and got in his face. "And just *how* do you plan to tame me?"

"There are ways. And I have so much privacy here. We're miles from the nearest neighbor. No one to hear your protests, my dear."

"You plan on beating me into submission? That's your plan? Might not be as easy as you think."

"Oh, I hope your screams of pain will turn to those of pleasure. There are many ways to elicit those. And I'm a master. I will be your master. You will be my slave and grow to crave my attentions."

She swallowed hard, refusing to allow him see how much he revolted her. Scared her.

How the thought of his touching her made her skin crawl.

"As soon as the minister leaves, your lessons in becoming a submissive wife will begin."

"That's what you think. Cord will come for me. He's a lawman—in case you've forgotten. He won't allow you or anyone else to treat me this way."

He grabbed her upper arm and dragged her down the hall to his room. "While we wait, why don't I show you what's in store...if you don't behave."

He shut the door behind them, locked it and slammed her against the door. Grinding his dry lips down on her mouth, he squeezed her breasts with his hands, kneading the tender flesh.

She bit back the cry of pain, refusing to give him the satisfaction. The pain distracted her for a moment then her anger flashed. She clawed at his eyes and jammed her knee upward. She wouldn't play his sick games.

Never.

He screamed, called her a vile name then jumped back, but her knee missed the soft targets she intended.

Grabbing her wrists, he threw her on the bed then walked over to an oak wardrobe and opened it wide.

Instead of clothing hanging inside, there were chains and leather implements of—hell-only-knew-what-instruments of torture they were. Only one was recognizable: as a leash and dog collar. "You will heel, sit, stand, lie down and spread your legs on command or you will be punished severely. Sometimes I'm told the pain is quite exquisite."

"You're a sick son-of-a—bitch—that's what you are."

He got down in her face, so close she could smell the Macassar oil in his slicked back hair. Her nose wrinkled at the obnoxious odor of the cigarettes he was so fond of smoking.

"And you are a self-indulgent little slut who nearly

gelded me when I merely tried to sample the bride I'd bought and paid for."

His hand snaked out and grabbed her breast through her dress and squeezed just hard enough she couldn't hold back a whimper.

"See what I mean. You liked it."

"Like hell, I did. Before I give myself to you, one of us will have to die."

The house maid entered the bedroom without knocking. "*Señor*, the reverend comes."

"Don't ever enter this room without knocking!" He aimed a kick in her direction, but she scurried away just in time. "About damned time." He grabbed Star's wrist and jerked her off the bed. "Come on. I've waited long enough."

"Ugh!" She hammered at his chest with her free hand and pulled back, but the bastard was stronger than he appeared.

Through the open door, she heard the sound of the minister entering the hacienda.

No.

Panic rose in her chest and threatened to cut off her breath. And the corset being so damned tight didn't help one little bit. "Slow down. I'm going to faint."

"Go ahead. When you awaken, you'll be married all the same."

When they entered the drawing room, the minister stood with his back to the room, staring out at the pack courtyard. He was tall and attired in an ill-fitted black suit, apparently a smaller man's castoff.

Then the minister turned, removed his derby and bowed low. His black hair was slicked back from his forehead, but his dark eyes shone with triumph. She stifled a gasp, but her heart fluttered like a bird's.

Cord.

She swallowed her surprise. He'd come. Should've known he would.

And about damn time!

Chapter Fourteen

"Mister—sorry, I'm no good with names—"

The man, who was a hair's breadth from being throttled, interrupted, "Theodore Darwin, Esquire! My name hasn't changed since we first communicated, Reverend."

"So sorry, Mr. Darwin. I presume this lovely lady is your intended." Star's eyes widened, the only clue of her surprise at seeing him. Unwilling, dressed and as yet unharmed. What more could a man what? He breathed a sigh of relief, even as he reined in the urge to flatten the uptight and oh-so-proper Easterner.

That weasel of a man thought he would make a suitable mate for a woman like Star? Apparently, stupidity and delusion ran rampant back East. Why he'd followed her all the way to Texas from Boston was what he'd like to know. She'd better have some answers, too.

"Yes, let's get on with it." The groom-to-be straightened his cravat. "You're half an hour late."

Cord dipped his head obsequiously, keeping up the pretense a tad longer. "Beg pardon, sir, but just before I set out this morning, my horse threw a shoe. Had to—"

"Enough! Say the words and get it over with." Darwin, as if he realized he didn't sound like a typical bridegroom, gave a sickly smile. "I mean, I'm just so anxious to make this lovely lady my wife." He held onto her hand tightly, making an obscene show of his affection.

Killing was too good for the bastard. Buried up to his neck in the desert with honey poured over his head—now that was more along the lines of a fitting punishment.

He eyeballed Star. "Ma'am, are you willing to marry this man, because I'm not so sure he's much of a gentleman at all."

Star jerked her hand from Darwin's grasp. Her bosom heaved with deep breaths and threatened to spill from their confinement. "I most certainly am *not* willing to marry him. I'd sooner marry a billy goat."

"I can see why that might be a problem. This man's a jackass if ever I saw one." He drew his pistol and shoved it into Darwin's pale face. "Lady doesn't look so willing to me. In fact, I'm of a mind to take her off your hands."

"How dare you!" Star's abductor opened his mouth and glanced over his shoulder.

"Don't waste your time looking or calling for your two bodyguards. They've been tied up and taken into my custody. You're here with only two men? I'd surely hate to overlook one."

"What about my brother? And Fields?" Star asked then pummeled Darwin's chest. "Did he really leave last night?"

"Fields?" Cord frowned. "Who the hell is Fields? And your brother's here, too?"

"Fields is a Pinkerton. Tom took me from the ranch and met up with Fields at the old hideout cave."

"No idea where your cowardly brother ran off to." Darwin's chin trembled. "Fields—he brought my fiancée here from her home and traveled quite some distance to do so. However he's no longer in my employ. Fired him for insubordination."

"Did you now?" Cord grinned.

Weapons drawn, Cord's two brothers eased into the

room. They quietly nodded. "Nobody left but the cook," Nash said, "and a terrified housekeeper. What do you want to do with him?" He jerked his head at Darwin.

"He goes back to Kenton Valley." He turned back to Darwin. "I have a cell ready for him." He got in his prisoner's face. "Just so you know, we Texans don't take kindly to having our women dragged from their homes in the middle of the night."

Darwin straightened his shoulders and stiffened his back, still stupid enough to think he could talk his way out of going to jail. "My betrothed came of her own free will. We were engaged whilst in Boston. This is all just an unfortunate misunderstanding."

Engaged? News to him. He leveled his gaze on Star. "You were engaged to this bag of bones?"

Her body stiffened and her face grew red. "He means he paid my mother for her permission to marry me."

"It was a contract. Very legal and binding. I saw to that myself. I am an attorney, after all." He puffed up with pride at the last statement. "You'd do well to remember that."

"Maybe you're a hotshot lawyer in Boston, but you're not in Boston anymore." Cord nodded at his brother. "Restrain him."

Nash jerked the prisoner's arms behind him and fastened the manacles, but the prisoner continued his protests, his tone growing shriller with each syllable. "My man brought her here. It was perfectly legal."

"With more than a little help from her brother who's gone missing."

"Wait," Star said and grabbed Cord's arm. "I don't care about my brother, but I think Darwin's men might've done something to Fields. When he brought me here and saw how Darwin really was, he promised he'd guard me through the night, but he was missing when I woke up this morning. Thing is he didn't strike me as a man who'd go back on his word."

"How about it, Darwin?" Cord gave the man a shake. "Where's your man Fields?"

"He's not Teddy's man," Star interrupted. "Fields is a Pinkerton agent. Old Teddy here hired him to bring me to him. Somehow Fields met up with my brother, and Tom's the one who took me from the ranch. Killed one of his own men, too. You probably already know that."

Cord nodded. "Yeah, I found the body."

"So where is he, this Pinkerton?"

"I told you." Darwin swallowed, and his gaze darted erratically. "I dispensed with his services. I suppose he left for the nearest train station to return back East."

Cord shook his head. "Damnation. I hate a liar. And something tells me you wouldn't know the truth if it bit you on the ass."

"Such crudity." The prisoner shook his head and whined, "I demand to be taken to Boston. I refuse to recognize frontier justice."

Aiming his six shooter at the prisoner's upper thigh, Cord leaned in close. "How about I start shooting body parts? Maybe I'll start with your knee joints. Keep stonewalling me. One more time, where's the Pinkerton?"

Darwin's throat worked; his body started to tremble. "Storage shed—next to the stable."

"Good choice." Cord smiled and put away his pistol. "You get to keep your knees, as long as you don't piss me off again."

While Nash and Luis dashed off to locate the Pinkerton, Star rushed to Cord's side and threw her arms around his neck. "You son-of-a-gun, it took you long enough to find me."

"I'm glad to see you, too, darlin'." He dipped his head and kissed her deeply. Her body softened against his then she stiffened and pulled back, her chin coming up a notch.

"I knew you'd come. I told 'em you would."

"Could've left me a better trail. Might've been here sooner. Didn't you have any bread crumbs?" he teased.

"Bread crumbs?" She set her hands on her hips. "Are you out of your ever-loving mind? First, my brother trussed me up like a pig in a poke and slung me over Dolly like he was taking me to market. Even after he brought me to the Pinkerton, my hands—"

He stopped her rush of words with another kiss. This time longer, deeper, hotter. Her hands played up and down the muscles of his strong back. "I was afraid you'd never find me—not in time anyway." She tiptoed and whispered so only he could hear, "Tom was here not an hour ago. Don't let him get away."

The Pinkerton was found and freed. He expressed his gratitude, and Cord allowed the agent to go on his way. The Pinkerton Agency was well-known and feared by many, and while quite a few of their agents were roughnecks and thugs, Fields appeared to be a man of honor. At least he'd protected Star to the best of his ability given the circumstances.

Cord and his brothers searched the entire house and every single inch of the grounds, but without discovering Star's brother. His horse remained in the stable, but that didn't rule out Tyler's having gotten away on a different horse.

The three men stood on the porch waiting for Star to change clothes. "Much as I hate letting him go," Cord said, "we need to hit the trail with this 'un. I can't wait to see him in my jail so he can stand trial for kidnapping." He nodded at Darwin, who'd finally shut his lying lawyer mouth. "We'll drop off his two guards in Llano. Sheriff there can do what he wants with 'em."

After what seemed like an eternity, Star emerged from the hacienda. She'd taken off the dress she was supposed to be married in and found something suitable for the ride home. And although he certainly enjoyed sight of her tits nearly popping out, he wasn't overly fond of the fact his brothers could, too.

Walking over to her mare, Star smoothed the folds of her divided riding skirt, probably wishing it was a pair of breeches. "Tom has to be here, and he deserves to hang for murder. Not that I didn't want to kill him myself more than once," she muttered then checked the cinches.

"Can't afford to wait any longer. Are you sure you're up to another day and night on the trail?"

She straightened, rubbing her back. "I'm stiff and sore, but I'm as anxious to get back home as you are." She glanced up at the sky, shielding her eyes with her hand. At that moment a shadow fell across her face. She frowned. "What—?"

A shot spit over his shoulder and close to Star's head. Cord shoved her to the ground and covered her body with his then rolled over, drawing his Colt at the same time and emptying it. Somehow he was vaguely aware of her scurrying for cover under the porch.

Tom Tyler teetered on the edge of the tile roof and slowly fell headfirst to the hard-packed ground below. Cord walked over to his body, kicked Tyler's gun from his hand and stared down into the bank robber's lifeless eyes.

Finally. The bastard got what he deserved. For the bank robbery that ultimately killed Cord's wife and unborn baby.

For abducting Star in the night and treating her like dirt all for a payday he hadn't earned.

Dreading her reaction, he turned and faced her. Her face paled to the color of chalk, her hands shaking. "I-is he...?" Her voice quivered.

He nodded. "Yeah. He's gone. Sorry. Didn't have a choice."

"He w-was shooting as us. Like he d-didn't care who he hit as long as he hit someone."

Her shoulders shook and she looked like her legs might give out any second. He slid his arm around her. "Darlin', you lost your brother a long time ago. Today just made it official." He clenched his jaw. "I didn't want to be the one who killed him. But it would've happened sooner or later."

"You'd rather have seen him hanged?" An edge gripped her voice, and she stiffened in his arms.

"Justice is justice, however it comes."

"That's convenient."

"No less true." Women. One minute she wanted to kill her brother herself and now she was pissed off because the deed was done. All right, so he'd told a half-truth: he had wanted to be the one to do it—just not right in front of her.

"It's not easy." She gazed up with teary eyes. "I don't know what to feel. I keep thinking back to when we were kids on the ranch. I don't know what happened to him."

"Started running with a rough bunch. They stayed drunk half the time, gambling, fighting. Next thing you know, he and his gang robbed a stage coach and never stopped to look back."

"He said you stole Annie from him."

"Damn fool. He wouldn't leave her alone. She was a gentle gal, didn't want anything to do with him and his wild ways. I kept an eye on her—that's sort of how we started keeping company. You were long gone. We just sort of fell into marriage."

She nodded. "I'm all right now. Let's go home."

Relief stole through his body and leached some of the tension. "You sure?"

"Yes. As long as we're all right?" She made it sound like a question.

"We are." He linked his fingers together and helped Star mount. Walking back to his stallion, he shook his head. Why the hell wouldn't they be all right? They'd just weathered him killing her brother. What else could go wrong after that?

Cord turned to his brothers who were staring at the horizon or their boots, anywhere to avoid the scene in front of them. "Wrap him up and tie 'im to his horse. Best get a move on before he ripens."

The ride back to Kenton Valley didn't seem as long or as arduous as the earlier trip. For this trip Star rode at Cord's side on her well-rested mare. Nash and Luis rode ahead with Darwin who, thankfully, was the one trussed up like a turkey instead of her. And her brother's body. Let her not forget that.

Only two days ago, her heart was light and her mind was filled with plans for their future. She loved this tall, handsome man even more than she ever thought possible. He'd saved her...from a horrible fate. Tied to Theodore Darwin for the rest of her life wouldn't have been a marriage. It would've been torture of the sickest kind.

Stop. This was no time to be thinking about Teddy Darwin and his wardrobe full of sick gadgets. Today was... She edged her mount closer to Cord's and grinned. "It's Sunday, isn't it? We were supposed to get married today." She said it softly and with a degree of shyness that surprised her.

A wry grin kicked up the corner of his mouth as he nodded in her direction. "Reckon the reverend will understand. When I formed the search party, the news spread pretty quick. Doubt he'll be waiting for us at the altar."

"No guess not." Biting the inside of her cheek, she cut a quick glance at her intended. "I hope Pa'll be home by the time we get there. He needs to know about Tommy."

He nodded. "Yeah, and about us."

She watched him shade his eyes with one hand and peer ahead. Was he trying to avoid looking at her directly? "We're still going to be married, aren't we? The preacher won't have forgotten how he found us."

Even without the threat of Teddy Darwin looming over her, she couldn't imagine being married to anyone but Cord.

"I'll marry you," he said. "I'm not the kind of man who goes back on his word."

"But—"

"Don't talk it to death." He kicked the stallion and increased their pace, riding several lengths ahead of her then turned in the saddle and said over his shoulder, "Let's get a move on. I want to make camp at the hideout cave before night falls."

"We *will* talk about it again," she called after him. "Just you wait."

Chapter Fifteen

"Just you wait."

Star's challenge echoed across the distance and, in spite of the heat, sent a chill dancing its way up Cord's backbone. When it came to getting her way, that woman was as relentless as a cowhand looking for a piece of pussy on payday.

Her eagerness for lovemaking had seduced him as surely as a baby seeks its mother's tit. No way would he deny her anything. He was bound to her. Bound by the spell she'd cast over him, not just since she'd returned from Boston, but years earlier when they weren't much more than kids.

The time they swam in the shallow river at the lower end of the valley, wearing near next to nothing. Star's breasts had budded almost overnight. What a fit her ma pitched that day. It was the end of summer and the end of swimming for Star. Her ma kept Star closer to home after that.

Whether it was the easy jostling gait of his horse, the memory of that day or both, his cock hardened like an adobe brick. He moved about in the saddle and adjusted his crotch.

Wouldn't do to cut off circulation. Given Star's partiality for his body parts, especially that one, she wouldn't appreciate a dickless husband. While not having a dick might be the solution to not getting her with child, he wasn't too anxious to see anything untoward happen to it, either.

The longer they followed the trail back to Kenton Valley, the more Cord acted as if she didn't exist. And the madder she became. She huffed and puffed her displeasure, and still that damn man kept several lengths ahead of her, no matter how she altered Dolly's pace.

The afternoon sun beat down even hotter than it had the day before. Perspiration dampened her neck and trickled between her breasts. Even worse, she smelled of horse. Not that a certain sheriff would let her get close enough for him to notice.

Fine. He could ignore her and punish her for wanting what any red-blooded woman would want. But once she had a ring on her finger and had him in her bed, things would change.

Damn right.

While they followed the trail back toward the Tyler Ranch, he managed to ignore Star's presence and bad mood. All right, he *tried* to ignore her. As soon as they reached the vicinity of the old hideout cave, he caught up to Nash. "Might as well stop here and make camp for the night."

She remained in a pissy mood, evidenced by her nose in the air and the scowls she shot in his direction. But she had smiles aplenty for his brothers, and they seemed to enjoy his discomfort. Damn woman was used to getting her way. But no way would he fall for it.

Hell no.

He watched as his brother Nash helped her dismount and tamped down his anger. He didn't care much for the way his traitor brother was simpering and smiling around her. A good talking to was in order for that one.

He walked over to where Star stood, shining her sweetest smile now on Luis. Couldn't she make up her mind which of the brothers she wanted? "How 'bout something to eat?" he asked, in an attempt to settle her down...and remind her just who she was supposed to marry.

She glanced up at him, squinted her eyes against the bright sun then pulled a prim and proper face. "No, thank you."

"You have to be hungry. I heard your stomach growling for the last five miles."

Her green eyes flashed with anger. "I don't see how you could have, and even if you did, how rude of you to mention it."

"Don't go all hoity-toity on me. " He leaned closer and said too low for Fields to hear, "Don't forget I've seen you wearing nothing."

"Appears you have an excellent memory, sir. I hope it'll keep you warm at night."

Cord scowled at Luis. "Don't you have something else to do—like water your horse?"

At this, his brother held up his hands in surrender and backed away from the scene.

Smart fellow. Knew if it came to blows, Cord could whip his ass with one hand tied behind.

He reached for her wrist. "Come on, darlin'. This ain't the time or place for you to get all bent out of shape."

She jerked her wrist from his hand. "If you're going to manhandle me, too, I should've just stayed in Boston."

Then she shook her head furiously. "No, I don't mean that. Not really."

"I know you don't. Eat some supper. Get some rest. You're worn out."

She glared at him, but her countenance softened a bit. Leastways he needed to think it did.

After a silent dinner, the men decided to take watches during the night. Cord stood and brushed the trail dust from his knees. "I'll take the first watch. I don't trust our Boston lawyer friend here. Likely he'll try to escape and get himself lost in the desert."

Maybe by the end of his watch, Star would be asleep and not capable of heaving more bursts of anger at him. He tossed his bedroll at her feet. "Here. You'll need this. Gets cold out here at night."

"Thank you." She fluttered her lashes and said softly, "You could keep me warm...if you were of a mind to do so."

Shaking his head, he let a smile come to his mouth. "I'm taking first watch. You get some rest. We'll leave at first light."

"It'll be good to get home." She nodded, but the way she held his gaze left no doubt what she wanted.

At least her mood had changed, even if her tune hadn't. He shut his eyes for a second and took a deep breath. The woman had one thing on her mind. And yeah, it was the same thing on his. He could almost feel the warmth of her, standing a foot away. And more than anything, he wanted to sink into that warmth and bury himself in her love.

But no.

Not tonight.

Not ever, except he'd be a fool to believe he would never take what was so freely offered.

*

It was midday Monday by the time they reached home. Star made out smoke coming from the bunkhouse chimney. Chuck was already cooking dinner for the hands who'd returned from the cattle drive.

She dismounted, and one of the hands took Dolly's reins and led the mare around to the stable. "See she gets a good rubdown," she called after him then turned to meet Cord's dark gaze. "Thanks for seeing me home, not to mention rescuing me. As you can see, the men have returned and I'll be quite safe. I'm sure Pa's around here somewhere."

He removed his hat, wiped the dust from his face with a faded blue kerchief. He shook his head and frowned, the sun glinting off his wavy blue-black hair. She itched to run her fingers through it...and a lot more.

"I have to ride into town and get my prisoner settled. But I'll be back to talk to your pa."

She nodded and stamped the trail dust from her riding skirt. "Will you be seeing the preacher? I've had a lot of time to think. No matter what he saw or thinks he saw, maybe we should just call off the wedding."

"Call it *off*?"

"I know I was all for it, but you were sort of forced into the position of saying we were affianced. Cord, I love you. Probably always will..." The words choked her and wouldn't come. How could she give up his love? His hands. His lips?

The lines at the corners of his eyes deepened as a puzzled expression took up residence on his face. "Tomorrow, first thing. I'll come back. We'll sit down and have a logical conversation. We'll make plans. Talk to your pa."

"I don't see what good it'll do." She set her hands on her hips, meeting his level gaze. "I want a real marriage."

His eyes narrowed, and his chin jutted forward. "Seems

we're at cross purposes. But your pa may have other ideas." He took a step toward her, the longing clear in his dark gaze.

Be strong. Let him go. She raised her chin, shrugged and scoffed, "Pfft. My pa and preacher don't have much truck with one another."

"Your pa will see the preacher about a decent burial for your brother. No doubt he'll hear we planned to marry."

"A lady is allowed to change her mind." She folded her arms across her chest. "And I've changed mine." Dammit. Why couldn't he just take the gift of freedom she was offering?

"That cow's already out of the barn. No matter what you say, your reputation's at stake." He loomed over her, his chest rising and falling rapidly.

Swallowing hard, she took a step back, but her heart hammered like a stampede. "This isn't Boston."

The second she uttered the words, the memory of her earlier visit to town hit her. Could she face that kind of disdain every time she showed her face in town?

His gaze narrowed. "May not be Boston, but we were caught out, and we're getting married. Make no mistake about it."

"Can't you get it through your thick cowboy skull? I'm letting you off the hook."

He grinned and his handsome face darkened under his tanned skin. "What you don't seem to understand is I don't want off the hook." He shook his head. "I know these folks better than you do. Kenton Valley is a damn small town. We need to be able to hold our heads up and face people. It's a matter of self-respect. I had no business getting you out of your clothes and playing around the way I did."

"There were two of us...playing around, as you call it."

Cord took another step forward. She took one back and

bumped into the porch column.

He grinned and circled her waist with his hands. "You're not getting away from me. You're going to listen." He leaned down and slanted his lips across hers. She tried to struggle, but with his hard body against hers, her knees weakened and a shot of heat darted to her core. He held her firmly, pressing her against the post, his cock jutted hard into her belly. She opened her mouth and allowed his tongue to battle with hers, while she started pulling his shirt from his duckins. He tasted of strong coffee. He roamed below her knees and pulled up her skirt. His ride-roughened fingers splayed over her thighs, pulling her closer.

Heat pooled in her belly. Damn the man. He knew the way around all her defenses. She loved him and that's all there was to it. All further conscious thought fled and was lost in the blast of a shotgun and a tree limb falling and a shower of leaves.

And an outraged roar. "Tarnation! You're no better than your ma."

Cord jumped back, damn fast and let her skirts drop. She quickly straightened them and smiled brightly.

"Pa—you're home."

Chapter Sixteen

Cord might be the sheriff, but he saw the glint of imminent death in old Buck Tyler's eyes. With a firm grip on his shotgun, the old man advanced on him, his bowlegged gait creaking from side to side, each step bringing death closer.

Being caught by the preacher was bad, but getting caught with his hand up Star's skirt by her bad-tempered, drunken daddy was a whole pile of shit worse.

She rushed to her pa's side. "Now, Pa, don't get all riled up. It—"

Tyler drew back his hand as if to strike his daughter. Cord stepped between the two. "Dammit, Tyler. Don't you dare lay a hand on her. We're gonna get hitched."

A cagey expression crossed Tyler's face as he rubbed his grizzled chin. "Reckon that puts a different light on things."

"Would've been married by now if she hadn't been taken."

"Seems like I heard something about that." Tyler whipped up the shotgun. "You the one what killed my boy?"

"Yes, sir. No choice. He shot at us. Nearly hit Star. But you need to know before your boy took his sister in the dark of night and brought her to a Pinkerton for a fee, he killed one of his own gang."

Tyler's pale eyes were watery and reddened. "That true, girl?"

"Yes, sir. The sheriff didn't have a choice. He saved my life. Tommy shot at us. Could've killed me. Not to mention he tied me up and hauled me off like a sack of feed. He and the Pinkerton argued about payment, so he finagled a way to get more money and helped the agent take me to Llano."

"Llano? Why the hell—?"

"Long story, Pa. This man from back East—he seemed to think I belonged to him."

"Did you?" Old Buck leveled his gaze on his daughter. "No bullshitting now."

"No!"

"How'd the sheriff come to know you were a-missing? You ain't been back that long."

Cord cleared his throat. "I—uh, I was supposed to visit Star that night. I found the body then formed a search party to ride after Star and your son. We planned to get hitched yesterday after church, but as she just said, she was taken by force."

"You couldn't wait to ask for her hand?"

"Sir, you were on the cattle drive to the railhead. We didn't want to wait."

"Someone else caught you with your hand up her skirts, did they?" He tried to laugh, but snorted and coughed instead.

"Don't be silly, Pa. You know I never wanted to go back East, but ma didn't give me a choice. I always wanted to stay here..."

"Because of this 'un?" He jerked his head toward Cord.

"Yes, sir."

Cord swallowed hard, still not too sure Tyler wasn't going to aerate his backside. "I love your daughter. I'll make her a good husband."

"'Til some sidewinder is faster on the draw than you are."

"I'm not a gunslinger. I'm a lawman."

"Same difference." He spat a stream of tobacco close to the toe of Cord's boot.

Might as well ignore the old fool's insult. "If you want to call the preacher, I'm prepared to marry Star right now."

"You will *not* marry me right now! My dress isn't ready." Star's face grew red as the sun setting on the cliffs. Her eyebrows were drawn together in a ferocious frown.

"Now, Star." He took her hand, hoping to calm her down and not piss off her pa any more than he already was. "I don't care if you marry me in those denim breeches of yours."

Her face flushing with heat and her green eyes shooting sparks like Independence Day fireworks, she jerked her hand free of his. "First of all, I've just been hauled all over Texas in the last three days, nearly suffered a fate worse than death—and Heaven only knows what else—by a man who thought he owned me. I'm tired. I'm dirty. And I'm fed up with all you men bossing me around and telling me what I'm going to do or when I'm going to do it. I won't get married in pants, and I will wear my new dress...as soon as it's finished."

More than a little buffaloed by her anger, Cord stared as she flounced back into the house. He glanced at Tyler. "I'd best go—"

"Nope. Reckon you might oughta let her cool down some. But you mind my words, there'll be a weddin' or a second funeral. One or t'other."

"Oh, there'll be a wedding. You got my word on that."

Tyler nodded. "Always heard you was a man could be trusted."

"You think—?" He nodded toward the house where a certain pissed off woman waited.

"Nah, not yet." He set the shotgun down by its butt. "Been a while since I was courtin', but if I remember correctly, women like to be asked—nice like."

"Already asked once, and she accepted," he said. The very thought of old Buck Tyler giving courting advice was enough to make him clamp his jaw to keep from laughing out loud. Likely the old coot wouldn't take it too kindly. Once he could trust he wouldn't break down, he managed, "Yes, sir. I'll try to remember."

He nodded and turned to find his horse. "Anyhow, I have to see to my prisoner. Already told her I'd be back tomorrow morning. Gotta see the preacher today, too."

Tyler nodded and spat. "See that you do."

Cord put his foot in the stirrup and swung into the saddle. Fine. Let Star stew for a while. Let her finish that dad-blamed dress. One of the many things he'd learned in the last five days was no matter how much trouble she was, she was worth it. He loved her—temper and all.

It wasn't the way she literally tugged at his balls as much as his heart. He'd nearly lost it when he thought he'd lost her for good. He reined the horse's head toward town and urged the animal forward.

Chapter Seventeen

The next morning, the sun dawned bright and hot in the sky. Star stumbled into the kitchen to start breakfast for her father. Chuck, the cook for the hands and trail drives, had already left a half-dozen eggs on the back stoop and taken the rest to fix breakfast for the men in the bunkhouse.

Once she had biscuits in the cook stove's oven, she leaned over and checked the ice box. Ice was getting low. She'd have to send Chuck into town for more. She pulled out the salted pork to fry up for breakfast.

Her father ambled inside. From the smell emanating from his boots, he'd come directly from the barn. She looked up from the skillet of melting bacon fat. "Take off those boots. You're tracking in heaven only knows what on my kitchen floor."

"You been up to no good while I was gone. Just want you to know I know. Preacher was scandalized."

She clenched her jaw and turned back to the skillet and broke three eggs into the fat and added several thick slices of salt pork. Damn that old fool of a reverend for being so nosy and talkative. Wonder how many more folks he spread that story to?

She pulled the pan of biscuits from the cook stove, scooped up the fried eggs, slid them onto a plate and slammed it on the table in front of her pa. "Here you go. Careful you don't choke on 'em."

Her pa grabbed her wrist. "Girl. You're trying my patience. Time you was married off to a man who's crazy enough to put up with your temper and foolishness."

She twisted her wrist away from his grasp. "And it's time you stopped drinking yourself into a puddle every night and saw to things on this ranch."

"You don't understand. You couldn't. Your ma leaving left a hole in me. Just trying to fill it only way I know how." He shoved a strip of bacon into his mouth.

"Bull!" She slammed the spatula on the counter. "Mama left because of your drinking."

"You don't know shit. She left me a long time afore she ran off and took you back East."

"Am I supposed to feel sorry for you?" In spite of her anger, a wave of sympathy flooded through her, surprising the hell out of her, too. She chewed the inside of her bottom lip while she tried to think of something to say. Something better than, "Sorry. Guess I only saw and heard one side."

He shot her an expression of understanding. "Your heart's not as hard as your ma's was, but if you don't marry that young man, you'll regret it."

"Don't you think I know it? But will he regret it in the long run? Not like he has much choice in the matter." As she voiced a fear that nagged her all night long, her bottom lip trembled.

So much for keeping her feelings to herself. Dammit.

She turned away and broke another egg into the sizzling bacon grease. Damn her pa for being such a man. If she never saw Cordero Tate again she'd...be just fine.

No, she wouldn't. She'd shrivel up and die an old maid. Tears welled in her eyes, blurring her surroundings. "You just—" She threw down the egg flipper and fled the kitchen, her father and her feelings.

But he called after her. "When he comes today or tonight, make peace with him—oh, and get busy working on that dress!"

She made it as far as the stairs before a smile tugged at her lips. The dress... Yes, she had to finish her wedding dress.

That same morning, Cord rode over to Reverend Moore's house. His wife admitted him. She was a short, stout woman, pleasant of face, but her beady, dark eyes were full of unspoken questions. Remembering his manners, he removed his hat. "Morning, ma'am. Need to see the reverend."

"You'll find him in the dining room, working on Sunday's sermon." She moved aside and gestured toward the back of the small dwelling. She cleared her throat. "I hear Miss Tyler's returned home. Is she recovered...after her ordeal?" Each pause was accompanied by an almost imperceptible lift of her gray brows.

"She's fine. Thanks." Damn busybody. Let her keep her questions to herself.

He tapped on the doorjamb. The reverend looked up from his task and gave him a smile of surprise, but a smile all the same.

"Good to see you, Sheriff. What can I do for you?"

"Star and I still want to marry. Thought Sunday after church, like we planned last week before..."

The reverend frowned, sucked a whistle of air through his teeth then asked, "Are you sure? I mean, considering what happened, no one would blame you if you had second thoughts...or perhaps wanted to wait an interval."

"I love her. And *nothing* happened." His face heated. Dammit, he hated having to say the words because it had been a close call. "She wasn't forced. My brothers and I— we got there in time."

"You're sure?"

"Very."

The reverend set down his quill and steepled his fingers. "There's another issue. This gentleman who had her taken from home, he called me to the jail last evening. He says he has a valid marriage contract. He's an attorney, so he should know."

"*She* never agreed to marry him." Cord tugged at the bandana around his neck, wishing there was at least a breeze. "The agreement was between him and her ma. Star's of age and she can't be forced to marry someone she doesn't want."

Hard enough time convincing her himself.

"He also says she assaulted him in Boston."

"Can't say as I blame her. You didn't see the contraptions he had in that house in Llano. Dog leashes. Whips. Chains."

The reverend sucked his teeth and paled. "And Miss Tyler has accepted your proposal of her own free will?"

"Yep." Dammit if this preacher wouldn't marry them, he'd find one who would if he had to ride all the way to Fort Worth.

The reverend sighed and picked up his quill. "Then Sunday it is. I'll let the missus know. She'll want to do something I'm sure."

Yeah, right, like look down her long nose.

"Appreciate it. See you Sunday." He turned and left the confined quarters of the minister's house.

Damn good thing she'd agreed to marry him, not with folks giving the stink eye for something that wasn't her fault.

It was late, past supper time, when Cord rode up to the Tyler ranch. Buck Tyler was sitting on the porch, fanning flies and nursing what looked like a good bottle of Kentucky bourbon. "Sir, you and I—we should talk. Sorry it took so long for me to get back. Matters came up."

Old man Tyler cleared his throat. "We already talked last time."

Star walked out onto the porch, wiping her hands on her apron. As far as he could tell, she was in a better mood. Calmer.

"You and her," Tyler said, jerking his head toward Star, "got to do the talking now. I'm going out to the stables, got to check on one of the horses. Got a warm joint troubling him. Might be a while."

Cord nodded his understanding and waited until Star's father was gone. "Might as well go inside." He opened the door and followed her inside.

"Fancy something to drink?" she asked over her shoulder.

At least she was feeling hospitable. Wonder how long the wedding dress would stand between them? He was dying to touch her, but didn't dare. No matter how dry his mouth, he shook his head. "No, thanks."

She turned and gave him a smile, one that warmed him all the way to his short curlies. The next second she was in his arms. "I'm so sorry. I guess I was just a little crazy yesterday. So much had happened."

"So you're not letting me off the hook?" He faked a hangdog expression then chuckled. "Damn good thing, since I already saw the reverend this morning and asked him to marry us on Sunday. Now that's if your wedding dress is finished and to your satisfaction."

She snuggled close and smiled up at him. "It will be."

For the second time in less than a week, he dropped to one knee. "Starlight Tyler, will you do me the tremendous honor of becoming my wife?"

"Oh, yes." Her eyes shone with unshed tears, and she trembled as she stood before him.

He got to his feet. "One more thing. Will you have my children?"

"What? Yes. Yes. Yes." Tears rolled down her face, and she turned her face upward for his kiss. He bent his head and met her sweet lips, slipped his tongue into her mouth and pressed her against the wall and ground his cock in her belly.

The back door slammed and they jumped apart.

Pa—never saw a man with worse timing. He stomped around in the kitchen then moseyed into the sitting room and stood in the doorway with his hands on his hips. "Well? Is it settled?"

Cord clasped her hand in his. She entwined her fingers through his and squeezed. He beamed down at her. "Your daughter has accepted my proposal, again, Mr. Tyler."

"Good." A big grin creased his weathered face.

Her pa actually smiled. Who knew the old coot could smile?

"So, when's the wedding? Think it oughta be soon, seeing as how the two of you can't keep your hands off each other."

"Sunday after church?" She gazed up at the man she loved with every bone in her body. "Is that soon enough?"

He gripped her hand even tighter and grinned even wider while his eyes glittered with desire. "No, but whatever you think best."

Her pa shoved his hands in his overall pockets. "Guess that'll do."

Cord nodded.

A measure of relief passed through her body, as if the weight of a full-grown steer had been lifted from not just her shoulders, but her soul. For the first time in weeks, she could breathe without worrying what was going to happen next. Cord loved her and would be a true husband. It wasn't about what anyone thought. Not really.

Pa cleared his throat. "'Spect Star ought to be getting herself to bed. You take care, Sheriff. The trail back to town's a tricky one."

Cord grinned and gave her a quick wink. "Guess that's my cue to head out and take my sorry self home."

"Guess so." Still holding tight to Cord's strong hand, she turned to her father. "All right if I walk him out?" Like she would've ever asked permission before. No point in tempting fate or her father's sudden good will.

"Don't dawdle too long. Wouldn't want to scare the horses." He snickered and headed back to the kitchen.

Cord slid his arm around her waist and pulled her snug into his side as they walked outside. "Can't say your old man doesn't speak his mind."

"That's for sure. But he likes you. That's plain to see."

"You know, he's not nearly as mean as his reputation."

"Well, I have to say he's softening a bit, and it's somewhat unsettling. I guess I was such a mama's girl that I didn't have much to do with him. He was busy running the ranch. Besides, Tom was always his favorite. But I have to say Pa's taking Tom's death better than I expected."

He shook his head. "What happened to Tom was

inevitable."

"I know. But I had a nightmare last night." She shivered. "Relived it all over again."

She stopped at the hitching post and patted the stallion's neck. The creature nodded his big head, pawed at the ground and snorted.

"He acts like he's more than ready to go home." She smiled up at Cord. "How about you?"

He pulled her into his arms and let out a long sigh. "Never ready to leave you, but your Pa made himself pretty damn clear."

"Sort of rude and smiling at the same time. I was thinking maybe you could make it out here for supper at least one night during the week. I don't think I can go without seeing you before next Sunday."

And since his prick was standing at attention, he probably couldn't either. She pressed against him and moved her hips from side to side, teasing him.

He groaned. "Got a feeling your old man is gonna be watching me careful like." He leaned down and nipped at her ear lobe then left a trail of kisses down her neck.

Her breathing grew ragged. He nudged open her thighs with his knee. She straddled his thigh and rubbed her naughty parts up and down. "No doubt." Her body burned to take him right there. "I need you, so much," she said with a rasp.

He lifted up her skirt and slid his hand down her dampening bloomers, found the aching spot and caressed it with his work-roughened fingers. Her inner muscles clenched as he inserted one finger then two, gently stretching her walls, all the while his thumb worked her clit in seductive circular motions. She gasped for air and reveled in the pleasure his touch brought.

"Come on, baby. Come for me. Your pussy's so wet.

You're close." He nipped at her neck and nuzzled her breasts through her bodice. With his free hand he unbuttoned the first few buttons and kissed the valley between her breasts then bit one of her nipples through the lacy chemise.

She arched her neck, and when she came, her entire body shook. Her walls gripped his fingers, and she kept thrusting and wishing it would never stop. A kaleidoscope of colors burst behind her closed eyes, and she sagged into him with a quiet moan. "If having your prick inside me feels any better than this...I'll probably die once we're married."

He slipped his fingers from her body and let her skirt fall. "Now for that you have to wait."

"What about you? Your Johnson is likely to bust out of your breeches." She knelt down in front of him and started fumbling with his buttons.

"Lord a-mighty, Star. Get up." He pulled her to her feet. "Your pa's going to come out here and shove his shotgun up my ass."

"Not if you shut your mouth and let me take matters in hand." She grinned and eased her hand inside his duckin trousers. She began to caress his length. "This would be so much better if you'd let me use my mouth on you."

"Woman, you have a mouth on you all right..." He lost his breath and let out a low groan as she gripped his cock and rapidly slid her hand back and forth along his rigid length until his entire body shuddered. His cock jerked and cum spurted into her hand.

He staggered then steadied himself by latching onto the hitching post. "Damn. You sure are a fast learner."

"What else could I do? You wouldn't let me suck you off." Grinning, she took her hand and licked his jizzum from her fingers, while he buttoned his pants. "Can't let it go to waste, now can I?"

"Lord a-mighty, I don't think you'll be the one dying. You'll probably fuck me to death before the first year's out."

She cast him her most quizzical expression. "I'm no expert, but is that even possible?"

"Hell if I know, but think of the fun we'll have trying to find out."

"I can hardly wait, and if you don't get on that horse right now, you might just find out this very night."

He cast a long, heated glance in her direction then swung up on the black stallion. She watched his back until she could no longer make out his tall form in the night. By all that wasn't so holy, being his wife would be pure heaven.

Chapter Eighteen

For Star the days until Sunday flew then dragged then flew again by turn. A rash of cattle rustling kept Cord too occupied to do more than pay a quick visit on Wednesday evening. She had to settle for a quick hug and a kiss that didn't last nearly long enough.

The day of the wedding ceremony was sunny and hot. Luckily the Sunday church sermon was short and sweet, and it seemed as if every blessed inhabitant of Kenton Valley attended, whether they were regular churchgoers or not.

Selma Nelson helped with the final fitting of Star's wedding dress of pale green cotton sprigged with tiny yellow flowers. The light green French lace trimmed the bodice, collar and cuffs. While it was a simple design, it was lovelier than any gown she'd ever worn in Boston. After all, it was her wedding dress, and a woman didn't get married every day.

Her pa attended in his best suit, clean shaven except for his thick, gray mustache. He kissed her cheek just before handing her over to Cord.

Miracle of miracles.

Cord's brother Nash stood up for him while his father and Luis looked on from the pews. After the ceremony,

Star suffered through the congratulations and knowing glances and too many glasses of punch to count. All she wanted was her handsome husband and a chance to get him out of his Sunday-go-to-meeting suit at the first opportunity and into their bed. At least a month would do, even though the reality was less.

His brothers promised on their lives not to call him for anything. Not even if Butch Cassidy moved to Kenton Valley and robbed the stage coach.

At last, sitting beside Cord on the buckboard, they put the church and the town behind them. She glanced up at her new husband and blinked back the tears trying to form then patted his knee. "We finally did it. We're really husband and wife."

"Damn straight we are. Just need to know one thing. Did you mean those words about honoring and obeying me?" His dark eyes shone with mischief and his mouth quirked up in a half smile.

Screwing her lips into a pout, she pretended to give his question great consideration. "Depends."

"Oh what?"

"Whether or not I want to."

"I see. Now I didn't hear any conditions in those vows in front of the preacher."

She let out a peal of laughter. Never had she been so happy or so in love. "I can't imagine what you mean."

"Need to know if you're going to be a dutiful wife. That's all."

A glimmer of what he meant hit her. "Will I perform my wifely duties? Oh, most certainly. And with great pleasure, I'm sure." Fluttering her eyelashes, she awarded him with her demurest smile.

They came to the fork in the road that would take them to her new home. She was anxious to see the house. He'd told her Wednesday night it was all cleared out, including his two brothers who'd moved into the bunkhouse at their pa's ranch.

Cord stared off into the distance, guiding the horse around a deep rut. She held on to the side of the seat. "You know, you might get tired of me. Wish you'd married someone else."

"Someone else?"

"Someone like—say, that Pinkerton fellow. He was a lot more polished than me."

"He never crossed my mind."

"Did mine. I got to thinking while we were in front of the preacher. What if a man like him suited you better than me and you didn't realize it until too late?"

"You were having doubts even during our vows?"

"Weren't you?"

"No!" Folding her arms, she gave an exasperated huff and moved to the far side of the buckboard seat.

"Now, come on. I wasn't having doubts about loving you. Just that you might be sorry later."

"Well, forget it. You're the only man for me, and that settles it."

"Glad to hear it."

"Tell me about the house. What's it like?" Were they going to sleep in the same bed where he'd slept with Annie? Why did she have to think of that now? It wasn't practical for him to buy a new bed just for her. No. Just erase those thoughts.

"You'll see it as soon as we come around the bend here. Nothing grand."

"It doesn't have to be grand. It'll be our home. That makes it special."

The buckboard dipped then righted again. She shut her eyes, gasped and held on tight. When she opened her eyes, she saw her new home. Two stories with freshly whitewashed milled siding. A porch ran across the front. A small pond was nestled near a tall cedar. As they wheeled around to stop in front, she made out the stable in the rear alongside a slightly overrun vegetable garden.

"Well?"

"It's beautiful, Cord." He'd built it for another woman, not Star, yet somehow she'd have to make it their home.

He hopped from the buckboard and held out his hands, then placed them around her waist and assisted her down ever so gently. Instead of kissing her, he frowned and rubbed his chin. "Uh, the house is aired and the bed linens are new. It's ready for my new wife." He cleared his throat. "There's nothing of Annie's left behind. I saw to that."

More and more uncomfortable, she shot him a grateful glance. "I feel like an interloper. Like maybe I don't belong."

Chapter Nineteen

Something else Cord had worried about during the vows. Might as well meet it head-on. "This is *our* home, Star. What happened before is over. Our home...where we'll have *our* family."

Without giving a warning, he scooped his new wife off her feet and climbed the two steps to the porch. She squealed, held on tight and buried her face in the curve of his shoulder.

He opened the door and carried her over the threshold. "Now it's official." He set her down.

"Welcome home, Mrs. Tate."

He dipped his head and kissed her hard, pulled her close and cupped her ass in his hands. While he rubbed her mound against his cock, he licked her lips, chewing on them. Sweetest, most generous mouth this side of the Rio Grande. Sweetest pussy, too.

"Think you need to see the bedroom right now, Missus."

"If you say so. See how obedient I am, so far."

"I'm relieved, though I didn't expect you'd decline."

"We do have some unfinished lessons, do we not?"

"Believe so, wife."

He swooped her up again and headed for the stairs. It was time to bury himself in his new wife and damn the consequences. And soon, 'cause his cock was about to burst the buttons from his breeches.

Bounding up the steps, he heated with the effort. Thank God, he'd left the upstairs windows open so the cross-ventilation would keep them a tad more comfortable.

He set Star on her feet. She glanced around the room then looked up at him, her full bottom lip trembling. "I'm gonna take this slow and easy. Don't be afraid."

"I'll never be afraid of you or anything you want to do to me. And you already know I'll do anything you want."

He clenched his fists for a second, almost afraid to touch her, this wife of his. No matter how many times he'd touched her before. Each time was like loving her anew. He started with the tiny buttons on the front of her dress. Slowly one at a time, he pressed a kiss as each bit of her fair flesh was revealed. She arched her back and moaned with each touch.

He eased the top of her dress off her shoulders and let it fall to the floor. Her full tits swelled above the lacy undergarment. He buried his nose in the warm valley between them and inhaled the fragrance: sweet, like some kind of flower. "Skin's soft as a baby's butt," he murmured. "And you smell so good."

"My pussy's getting wet. Think you could move up the pace a bit?"

"Your pussy's wet? Now how'd that happen? I better check." He reached under the full skirt for her mound and massaged her clit through her bloomers. "Yeah, you're wet all right."

He removed his hand.

"Don't stop," she said with a squeal, but stood there allowing him to take his time all the same.

"We got all night, darlin'." He unlaced the lacy booster thing. "This is sure some contraption. Not sure I approve.

Might make a man want to do dangerous things to his wife." He slipped it off her shoulders.

Finally. Those firm tits with their coral tips were his and his alone. "Mighty nice they are, ma'am." He weighed one in his hand and felt the firm heft then latched on to the other breast and sucked the nipple into a tight, round bead and grazed it lightly with his teeth.

His wife moaned and sagged into his arms. "I need to lie down."

He chuckled, loving her responsive body. "Not yet." He unbuttoned her skirt and let it fall then slipped the petticoat over her round ass. Next off with the danged bloomers. He jerked them down, and she stepped out of them, kicking them to the side while she bit her bottom lip.

Her entire ever-loving body was on display for him alone. The thick red thatch of crisp curls where her slim ivory thighs joined was enough to send a man straight to heaven.

Soon he would part those thighs and make her his wife for real. Just like she wanted. A man couldn't live his life in fear. Not if he was a real man.

"It's my turn," she told him with a saucy toss of her hair. "First, this silly tie. Did I tell you just how handsome you looked as I walked down the aisle?" She shook her head and loosened his cravat. "No, I didn't. But the sheriff was looking mighty fine. And do you have any idea of the naughty thoughts I was having? 'Course not. You would've blushed." While unbuttoning his shirt—too damn slowly for his liking—she pressed her mound against his cock and gave a little wiggle.

"Whoa, baby. Careful." Shards of lust spiked from his balls to his prick. Not that it wasn't already hard enough to nail a board, much less the woman before him.

"So touchy." A delicious giggle emitted from her sweet

throat. Finally. She yanked the shirt tail from his trousers
and slipped his shirt and jacket off his shoulders at the
same time.

"Mm. I like these hard muscles—a lot. Cowboys are so
much nicer than lawyers that way."

Startled, he grabbed her wrists and held on tight. "Just
how many lawyers' chest have you seen, Missus?"

She struggled a bit. "None like this, but old Teddy was
fond of pulling me close—just like you are right now, I
might add."

He dropped her wrists. No way would he ever act like
that miscreant.

"I could tell he was soft and his belly was flabby." She
shrugged. "Those were the least of his faults. Besides, I
don't want to think about him when I'm standing here
naked as the day I was born and you're still half-dressed."

"I'll rectify that mighty quick." He hooked a thumb in
his belt buckle and unlatched it while Star's fingers were
nimbly unbuttoning his pants.

Within no time, he was as bare as she was. She gazed
upward, her green eyes darkening into the shade of
emerald gemstones and glittering with desire. "This time,"
she said with a quiver in her voice, "you'll really make me
your wife?"

"Damn straight I will. Enough talking." He picked her
up and settled her on the bed.

With his face so close Star could make out every sun-
drenched line, she slipped her arms around his neck. "I
love you, Cord. I've loved you ever since the last summer I
swam with you and Tommy."

He grinned down at her. "That long?"

"You're supposed to tell me how long you knew you

loved me."

"Is that how this works? You talk and tell me what to do? Not sure that's how it's really gonna work."

Straddling her, he crushed his lips down on hers and stole her breath away. She opened her mouth to his. His tongue swept inside and battled with hers, while his hands kneaded her breasts. Her nipples tensed into tight nubs of almost painful sensations that threaded through her belly to her pussy. Already she could imagine him filling her. Loving her.

Then he slid one hand between her thighs. She parted to give him better access. He inserted one finger then two, stretching her maidenhead even more than he had before. Her inner walls clenched his fingers as she arched her hips. "Now I want you. I want your cock inside me."

"You talk so bad." His voice rasped harshly in her ear. "What am I to do with such a wife?"

She levered up on her elbows. "Don't you dare spank me."

"Tell me what you want, baby."

"I want your big prick in my—you know."

"Say it. Say the dirtiest word you know for your 'you know'."

If her husband wanted her to use bad words, who was she to say him nay? "Pussy. I want to feel your cock in my pussy. Now."

"We've played around a lot. Still might hurt a bit, though."

"Don't care. Shove it in." She grabbed for his cock. The head glistened with a drop of cum. She wiped off the pearly droplet with her thumb and put it in her mouth, tasting the barely salty fluid.

His fingers inside stretched her inner walls again then he pulled them out and rubbed his cock with her moisture.

Positioning himself over her, he rubbed his cock up and down her slit. Her inner muscles contracted again at his mere touch. He held her shoulders while she opened her legs wide and arched up to meet him. He thrust home, hard and deep in one swift, sure stroke.

She gasped and tensed at the initial pain and, for a brief second, tried to retreat.

He held her fast by her shoulders. "No. Breathe in and out," he said. "It'll get better."

She did as he said, and sure enough, her body began to relax and adjust to his length and breadth. At last he was hers. Hers to love and lie with every night for the rest of their lives.

Slowly he began to move inside her, easily at first then straining upward with each stroke. Catching on to the age-old rhythm, she locked her ankles around his waist and met him stroke for stroke, gripping his broad shoulders for leverage. Each deep thrust filled her with wonder as their bodies slapped together.

Filled her with his heat. And most of all, filled her with his love.

His mouth on hers, their tongues battled. His lips hard then soft. Her hands fisted in the sheets, her body flushed with heat from the exertion of taking all she could get of his loving. And marvelous waves of sensation centered in her pussy and grew until her inner walls clutched his cock. When she could stand it no more, she crested the final wave and exploded with a burst of color behind her eyes. She called out his name with tears in her eyes.

Cord was truly her husband, and never would she ever love another.

His hips pumped and he drove into her body with a shuddering cry and collapsed to her side, careful not to crush her with his weight.

When she could finally breathe again, she brushed away the damp curls from his forehead. "Was I all right?"

Cord gazed over at the only woman he had ever loved...or ever would...and grinned. "Damn near perfect, I'd say."

"And we can do it every night? Just like we did tonight?" She chewed her bottom lip. "And you're not worried about me having a baby?"

He shook his head. "Darlin', I'll always worry about you, especially when you get with child. But being around you has shown me living in fear isn't much of a life. Or much of a man."

She giggled and twisted a lock of hair around her finger. "Think there's no doubt about how much of a man you are. Plenty of evidence of that here tonight. Would you be upset if we've already made a baby?"

He gave her a long kiss. "No. And if we have, I'll take real good care of you both."

"Kiss me like that again, and you're gonna have to take real good care of me right now."

"How did you get to be such a wanton woman?"

"I don't think I'm wanton, unless you mean I'm wantin' some more of your lovin'." She kissed him back, until his cock hardened again. "Then I'm definitely wantin' more of my new husband." She reached between them and held his cock in her hands. "I think he wants me, too."

He let out a chuckle. "And you'd be right, wife." What else could he do? He loved her with his mind. His cock. And with all his heart.

The End

About the Author

Marie-Nicole Ryan was born in a small western Kentucky town, but after college and marriage, she said "Good bye" to small town life. After spending three years as an army wife, she landed in Nashville, TN, where she spent several decades working as an R.N. and case manager. Finally in 2002, she achieved her lifelong dream of becoming a published author.

She loves all lawmen and detectives and writes erotic historical western romance and contemporary romantic suspense. TOO GOOD TO BE TRUE, won a 2008 EPPIE for erotic romantic suspense. In addition, her mystery/suspense novel, ONE TOO MANY, was a 2009 EPPIE Finalist.

She returned to her old hometown in western Kentucky in 2010. When she's not slaving away at her current work in progress, you might find her walking her dog Kelsea, a Sheltie rescue, or at the Y. But you won't ever find her in an airplane. No, not ever.

She's a former member of Romance Writers of America® To learn more about Marie-Nicole Ryan, please visit her web site at marienicoleryan.com. To keep up with her latest releases, new, and contests, send an email to Marie-NicoleRyanNews-subscribe@yahoo.com

Or you may follow her on:
Facebook: https://facebook.com/marienicoleryan.author
Twitter: @MarieNicoleRyan
Web site: https://marienicoleryan.com